THE BOOK OF DEVASTATION

~ A COLLECTION OF LIFE EXPERIENCES ~

CHRISTOPHER JAMES BINGHAM

MINDSTIR MEDIA

Published by Mindstir Media, LLC
45 Lafayette Rd | Suite 181| North Hampton, NH 03862 | USA
1.800.767.0531 | www.mindstirmedia.com

Printed in the United States of America
ISBN-13: 978-1-960142-44-3

CONTENTS

A LETTER FROM THE AUTHOR

Hello, my name is Chris Bingham, and I began this creative writing from a journal I started in 2017. It consists of many fiction and non-fiction writings and some true stories of my own life and dreams I have had. I wanted to share this book to teach kids and students that your dreams are possible and that any writing can be important to the universe. That goes for poetry as well.

Don't throw it away because you never know who might need to hear it. Possibly someone 500 years from now will read this and it may be just what they need to see and hear at the time. I insist the reader keep an open mind because some of the writings might sound a bit un real but I have come to learn that in our universe, anything is possible.

I trust you will like what you read and may even bring about some laughter, so please do enjoy my first master piece. Also, I might add, that I got the idea for this book from a book of short stories and poetry that I had once read in high school. Without further a due please enjoy these stories of a lifetime. Thank you...

MY MERLIN CAT

When I was a young boy about 5 years old my Aunt Chrissy had a cat for me to take care of while she was away overseas serving in our nations Navy. I named the cat Merlin a nice dark, gray, almost blue colored alley cat. Me not being much of a cat person, but an animal lover of all, knew there was something special about Merlin. In all my year's I have never met a cooler, better, easier to take care of cat than Merlin. He took care of himself. He lived outside so I would bring him his food and water every morning and afternoon at around 5 o'clock. My family and I were poor at the time so it was a big deal that we made sure to feed him, so no food would go to waste. Plus Mama didn't want him coming inside for whatever reason.

I would follow that cat anywhere and one time the cops found me in a bush down the street with Merlin. My mom was having a fit because I was young and she didn't know where I had wandered off to. Mom was worried and didn't know I was just chilling with Merlin and had plans on going back home. The cop gave me a ride home and it pleased my mother that he had found me. Mother was just glad I was okay.

The next day I sat out front around 5:00 p.m. the time when Merlin usually would come to visit and eat his dinner. Now Merlin lived outside even overnight but he never missed a meal. He needed his food for energy so he could do more sensible prowling. I knew this about Merlin and he always showed up for dinner. This evening he did not show. For the next two week's I waited out front for him but he never came back to get his food after that day. I was sad and worried he got hurt in a raccoon fight or even worse ran over by a car. After a few weeks of waiting, and Merlin not showing up, I gave up on him coming home and had no choice but to go on with my life. I soon got a dog named Gizmo after Merlin went missing. He was my dog for the next fourteen years. He was my pride and joy. I love dogs because he loved me back., plus he didn't go anywhere like Mooch does. Mooch was special.

When I was most of the way grown up, and going to high school I met my best friend Colon who lived ten blocks from the house I grew up in with Merlin. Not even ten blocks more like six blocks. Anyways the first time I ever went over to visit Colon at his house, I was walking around the side and into the backyard to knock on the door like I was instructed too, and a cat with a big old rat in his mouth greeted me there. Colon's mother loved cat's like my aunt and I did. Ironically enough the cat was a dark gray color and looked just like my old cat Merlin from when I was just a boy. At the time I thought "nahhhhh couldn't be….." Mind you this is like 12 years later. Colon answered the back door and said "ahhh, so I see you've met Mooch!" Cats for whatever reason don't always like me but Mooch and I got along from the get go. He always greeted me by rubbing up against my ankles in a figure-eight motion. He was an old bud-wiser ally cat who lived to be 26 years old. His nose was always all scratched up and quite often had dried up blood around his face and ears from fights in the neighborhood with squirrels and raccoons. The crusted up old blood didn't seem to bother anyone but me of course, and after a while I got used to the fact that that's was just how Mooch rolled. Dirty old alley cat nowadays.

On hot summer days Mooch would chill inside with the rest of the neighborhood kids, Colon, and I. See I found out later that Mooch really liked it inside too, because he was a straight bad ass alley cat, but I think he must have had a problem with Mom not letting him inside, so he went along down the road to the cat lady's house, whom son I became best friends with, Colon. So on hot summer days Colon would leave the faucet in the kitchen running just enough to slowly dribble some water for Mooch. Mooch could then drink leaking water out of the kitchen faucet like a water fountain. It took me until some years after Mooch died at 26 for me to connect the dots and realize Mooch was MERLIN!!! When I did realize it, I knew I would have to write Merlin's story for him in all his glory and due respect to the greatest cat that ever lived, my favorite cat in the whole wide world by fat and far! He was a skinny ole thing too.

Colon's mother had been feeding him too. Mooch was the bad-ass cat in the neighborhood and had scratch's all over his nose from fighting rats and racoons but Mooch, excuse me Merlin, never died or lost a fight, or got ran over by a car, he was just being spoiled by the greatest cat lady on the block Colons Mom, my whole life, only to be re-united with each other years later when I was in high school. He hadn't gone far and I was just happy to know he lived a good fulfilled cat life and was well taken care of by my great family friends Colon and Justin and their mother and father. We were all spiritually connected and it was Merlin's way of introducing us to our spiritual purpose of being in each other's lives. We're all family. Namaste.

Merlin was re-named Mooch because he mooched off the other cats food laid out on the patio at Colon's house, plus he had other cat friends there to play with as well. Merlin-Mooch lived to be 26 years old and literally was the coolest cat I ever knew and saw a true bad-ass of an alley cat. Sometimes I think Merlin was connected to God and had moved over there for a reason since I don't believe in coincidence. God works in mysterious way's that's for sure like an ole alley cat per say.

Colon and I turned out to be best friends before high school was over and had a lot of great memories in that back yard with Mooch and even recorded some of the greatest rap songs known to man in the garage where we smoked our pot and let Mooch watch over us. I was there little beer mooch, but I always am sure to return the favor. Like my friend once said, "you scratch my back and I will scratch yours." Makes sense in my mind, isn't that what friends are for....

DON-DA-BACK

One-night, a long time ago, about the turn of the century, in 1901 a man was out hunting gators in a small lake in NW Florida. He was stunned when he caught himself staring at a 14-foot alligator.

He grew up on that lake and was raised up fairly-well on how to hunt gators in the area. He had a father who taught him well. Things like how to snap snake's necks by the rattler, flinging it like a whip. He would also fish for big gator meat to feed the family for months out of the year. He especially liked to hunt late at night around midnight when gators are most hungry and active.

He knew Big Bertha lived out there and was afraid of her. You can see their eyes gleaming in the moon light at night. Moving slowly across the top of the still glassy like lake water. This is a medium sized fresh water lake that many of the gator's families had inhabited. Big Bertha was the mother of all and the one gator who had the most respect.

Don the gator hunter had two brothers and a much older mother and father. His job was to always keep food on the table for the family. Gator tail, gar meat and fresh water cat fish seemed to be his specialty. They always had enough to get through each season with the resources he would gather throughout the year on that lake. Life was awesome and they all got so good at there specialty areas of work that they rarely ever had any problems except for maybe struggling a bit to stay warm in the winter.

The lake was surrounded by trees on all sides of the egg-shaped lake. They only had two other neighbors who inhabited the lake with them way back then. Needless to say it was pretty thick kind of country. Full of large live oaks, Cedar, Pine, and what I like to call Paper trees. Lots of frogs would croak loudly at night and the mosquitoes would keep you awake, until the crickets hummed you to sleep.

It was the beginning of winter and Don had already burned through the first yard of wood that year. It seemed staying warm in the winter was one of the hardest tasks to grasp. He does his hunting for gator in the summertime and had a good year, so they had plenty of meat to eat but keeping enough wood and staying warm that cold winter wasn't easy.

Don and the family knew how to survive and manage through hard times since they had all lived in Odessa, Florida their whole lives. Growing up wasn't easy. Life was working to survive and live off the land, but it was a good life.

Late one cold night the last of the wood in the stove burned up quicker than expected. Don figured they would have made it through the night but unfortunately that wasn't the case and they were all slowly freezing at around midnight.

Don did the only thing he could do and went on a late-night search for firewood in the most wooded trail he knew, down by the lakes shore and edge. He knew better but it was late in the night and he was tired and cold and only thinking about staying warm, that he forgot that this neck of the woods belonged to Big Bertha, a 14-foot cannibal alligator.

It was her feeding time. She laid quietly and still in the wiregrass right across the trail from a fallen oak tree. The same oak tree Don had his mind on for chopping up firewood from it. It was there best source of wood and although Don had plans to go in the morning when the sun came up, he had to keep his family warm through the night.

Not even thinking about Bertha's territory he came rifling down the trail, towards the tree, where Bertha was waiting on her prey. He did not see Bertha and it happened so fast that it was to late, all he heard was "whoosh, snap!" real fast, "slash, crack," and Bertha had Don by the left leg. Like walking into a bear trap but worse, Don was completely frozen in that moment when he realized he forgot about ole' Bertha and that being her spot and all. He knew he was in deep trouble and probably would not make it out alive.

Big Bertha thrashed and threw big six foot, two-hundred-pound Don on the ground like a rag doll. Don knew there was nothing he could do to fight back, but instead, go limp and hope and pray to Jesus, Bertha would let him go, so he could crawl away but that wasn't the case. Big Bertha had dinner plans that night Don knew nothing about. Bertha dragged Don's ass right down into that dark murky water. She had a nice tree stump picked out for Bambi, but it seemed Don made it just in time for her dinner date.

Bambi must had been running late and it seemed Big Bertha wasn't to picky after all those years of watching Don stab, shoot and gut her babies. No wonder this was more than dinner for Bertha this was a reckoning.

Don barely alive, was then stuffed roughly up under the stump underwater to drowned and marinate for a later in the day dinner date with Bertha.

Don unaware that Big Bertha was so big because she was a mutant alligator with some sort of mutating disease in her saliva, gums, and teeth. Don thought, "this is it I'm going to die..." He then started severely shaking and shuttering, underwater and under the stump. He began mutating into something other than himself. First, he got bigger, and then stronger, and let me remind you Don was already a big man. Six-foot-tall and two hundred pounds to be exact.

He then turned a dark forest green. Grew a short, rounded snout and sharpened teeth like an alligator. Don lost his hair and now had the thick green skin of a gator. His spine even began poking up through the skin. Ripping off the bloody clothes, his alligator claws seemed to be the final stage of his horrifying mutation.

Now standing eight-foot-tall, with green skin, an alligator snout, webbed claws, and a brand-new alligator tail. Don was now Don-Da-Back! His mind was not the same, he now had a taste for blood. But not just any blood, gator blood. This was his lake now but first he would have to get rid of Big Bertha. He also noticed the sweet sensation he had for human blood, something he will have to overcome later, if he ever wanted to see his own family again.

He swam to the lakeshore and there in the pale moon light out of the dark murky water arose Don-DA-Back! He let out a hissing, and screeching howl waking all the creatures in the forest including the neighbors and his own family. Dawn was arising and so was his family. His brother Steve was the first to notice his absence in the morning. Worried, Steve set out to look for him. Steve was familiar with this neck of the woods and followed Don's tracks over to the scene of the struggle.

All he found was Don's bloody clothes torn to shreds. Not giving up hope he searched the rest of the day for his brother and when he didn't find Don, Steve had to tell Mom and Dad the tragic news. They were all distraught and left in grieving pain that week.

What Steve didn't know was that Don was hiding in the trees watching his brother, doing his best not to attack him. Don wanted to get used to the smell of a human without wanting to eat him, for Don was still hungry after the mutation and soon would hunt down Big Bertha. He would eat her in vengeance only to make him more powerfully mutated than any man or alligator. Half man and half alligator. He has every advantage with a human brain and able to walk on two feet.

Gracefully, he humanly remembered how to hunt a gator with bait, line, and a trouble hook. Not as humanly smart as he was, Big Bertha still did not stand a chance. He now not only had the smarts to hunt and capture Big Bertha, but the power and strength to wrestle, catch, kill and eat her like the true cannibal gator he shall become.

Starving nearly to death, Don set up his bait by her lair and found a nice nest to chill in, while he waited upon her arrival. The neighbor's dog was easy to catch and use for bait when your half man, half alligator. Don-Da-Back was preparing a meal best served cold.

Just as Don-Da-Back expected right around 5:00 p.m. in the sunny afternoon, Bertha showed up and ate the bait and swallowed his hook. She went into a death roll but posed no match for Don-Da-Back at this point. With his trusty field knife the moment she stopped rolling Don-Da-Back jumped on her back and stabbed his field knife deep into the back of her head piercing through and into her brain. Killing her.

She stopped rolling in a second and it was all over. Don-Da-Back had his feast. Stuffed and fully mutated Don-Da-Back was now stronger then ever. This was now entirely his lake to live on. He saved her carcass as an over-coat to scare people, poacher's, and intruders. Stories of Don-Da-Back have now been passed down through the ages.

Don's family was devastated. Steve went back out the next day to search for Don. Don-Da-Back knew that Steve would be looking for him. He waited patiently for Steve to let Steve know what had happened and how it will be from there on out.

As Steve showed up, he heard a rustle in the bushes, he stopped and waited quietly. Slowly Stepping out from the trees, Don-Da-Back revealed himself to his brother. Slightly taken back and gasping for air, Steve looked and stared and said, "Don is that you?" Don groaned with a sigh, "yaaa it's me Steve…" With a deep growling voice. Steve asked, "What happened?" Don said, "I think you know." Steve said, "okay, yes, I can tell,

I've never seen anything like this before in my life." "What should I do?" asked Steve. Don said, "tell my story and warn people of me!!! As he took back off into the woods releasing a loud, screeching scary, yet sad howl!!!

Steve did as Don asked and told his parents the story of what happened. Nobody believed Steve but he knew it was true. Steve kept the greatest myth of the lake close to his heart. He also had the best camp fire story to tell the kids and parents who visited the lake. Sometimes Steve would even dress up like his brother to scare the kids and make everyone laugh. It gave some light to a truly horrific story. The kids loved it and so did the parents. The warning Don gave, was a very real warning, even today.

The last I heard the mutation had made Don-Da-Back an immortal and is still alive in those woods today over a hundred years later. There are stories of sightings, and some attacks over the years, but nobody really knows where Don-Da-Back stays, not even hunters. For Don-Da-Back is the woods.

LETTER TO GOD OUR FATHER

Honestly, I write this with all shame set aside. I think I may have been taken hold by a demon only you can save us from. Half my face is blue and the other half pure light. It seems the two are in ka-hoots because I have been feeling a lot of negative vibrations and have developed I slight shake from it. I have seen it rear his ugly head in my dream one night and I had no idea it was quite like that. Looks like death. I have been used but I also stuck the needle in my arm myself, even the first time I asked to do so. I let my curiosity get the best of me. I am not completely the same as I once was but know how we can fix it together. I know how pure of heart I am and was only trying to help and didn't understand what this was. Is it true the things I believe as my past life? I believe so. Maybe not all of it but most. Help is what I need. I have received the holy talisman of St. Michael which has been good to me. I am nothing without GOD and grace. I have become an addict and alcoholic yet kind at heart, I have no control over this disease. Sometimes I do but I fall short since the main difficulty lies in my mind. I know how good, and beautiful my heart can be. I am foolish for allowing myself to be deceived.

To thine own self be true. I was thinking maybe I shouldn't have accepted this world for how it is and stayed close to home and not gone out into the world. My love, compassion and curiosity got the best of me so I learn to repent.

I am cold and desensitized by this world and know it's not the right place for me. I'm not stupid just a little foolish at times. I play foolish. I wake up crying and can't sleep. I took advice no fool would take out of some deep trust inside of me like a feeling of love that needed to be shared not just to prove a point but that I am willing and caring enough to give you the shirt off my back. Unknowingly and unwittingly I see people as just people and would never expect such manipulation, deception, delusion, etc. in my life. I want to see you and hug you again one day. My pride and my ego is not always my amigo and can get a little carried away. I find a sense of love when I practice humility.

I repent for my sins. How else should I do it. Maybe go see a priest. I will go by the river and jump in and holler. I want to do something I have never done before. I also want to abide and be as obedient to your will as possible. I have struggled a lifetime battling my own addiction and am at a loss overwhelmed and begotten. Didn't realize it was quite like that until I had a spiritual awakening. All the training in the world couldn't have prepared me for that. I knew drugs were bad but not like this. My fear is not real and my fear is without faith. Help us God I'm not the only one there are lots of sinners like me I just got it bad. Is it true? Did I somehow sign my life away without even knowing. I was deceived. I make mistakes, fall short, and can be unwilling sometimes but in person I always do as I'm told. Sometimes I hear spiritual voices and noises and it makes it hard to differentiate but I am getting better at knowing the truth. I'm exhausted but today I vow to not give up or let myself down anymore. Frothy emotional appeal seldom suffices. All I can do is do it. Pray continuously and get through it. Amen I love you Jesus whoever, wherever you are. I see your picture and we look a lot alike. You are a great example and could be a real live master in my life.

I am a child of God my creator. The Lord's prayer I say. I'm not perfect but I was at some point in my life. My sinful ways are not of my true nature. I made the mistake of believing in only the light. I was naïve. Accepting this life as I went on as just something for people to have fun with. It ruined my life but through Christ who strengthens me I was able to re-build my life into a very nice little, humble habitat. Unexpectedly I had lots of fear and very little doubt. I was too eager to reach out-ward. My life is good only because God is so great. I have many questions about who I am yet you have revealed most of them to me already. Thank you. I'm a great follower. I could use a hug been kind of lonely down here. Will be good to re-unite with our father. It has been a long journey but a good one. Thanks for not leaving me or forgetting me.

A VISIONARY

have had a vision of how the universe we live in today was created. A theory of mine and I don't know why I choose to write about it except for that it may seem interesting for one kid in the future. There may have been a big bang and the only thing left was five spirits and her stardust scattered throughout space.

It was the end to an old universe and the birthing of a new one. I had an idea, why not try to convert enough energy from the universe to never have to start over again. And so we did. Four spirits who introvert and gather stardust, and one creator who makes it real and possible into what we see today. This is just a memory or an idea a theory. I was most successful in gathering the most stardust and energy we know now as our sun a.k.a. the bright morning star. In the Bible it is written to be true but I don't know how accurate my story is.

I simply introverted myself in the shape of a sea horse or shrimp in a black abyss of star dust, taking in as much energy as possible and helped create enough power to last an entire eternity. If on a scale you measured the amount each of us had gathered I was off the reichter scale. Basically ton's more than what the others had gathered and I earned my spot as number one out of the four. Beautiful everlasting life eternal. All I now have is this eternal moment that I love to live in and will take life however I can get it because it is good raw emotionless hue's on love and life.

My creator uses the energy and stardust we gather out of left over space to then re-create me in power, a human being, to start a new life. Since I gathered the most star dust GOD creates me first and I only have an idea on how that is done. It's done by the spirit of man but not sure how. I love a good unanswered question. Everyone always wants to be first but I like to believe there's a reason why I win because I don't believe anyone would do it quite like me. I see the greater good and lookout for the people in it. Love and compassion is more important and necessary to human life than survival itself. God is my father and our lives are one and all supposed to be good. Namaste. I only wish to create a life filled with joy, love, and abundance for all of mankind. Let there be light.

Then after that it's time to meet one another. I manifest first then two, three, and four and so on. Then we get to meet our better half the stardust in which we need each other. I believe there's two sides to every story right and same goes for this one. There's the spirit then there's the power or the star. The greatest spirit chooses me the greatest star kind of a no brainer. We must learn to love one another and co-exist which sometimes is easy and sometimes it's a little more difficult but all in all it will always work out exactly the way it should. What is God? I choose to call GOD love. What would the universe be like if it was something that doesn't care for others and the things in it. And yes she is uniquely beautiful the one. I can still see her now for the first time, I was awe stricken. Love at first sight. Soul mates.

I promised her a life fulfilled and by golly I keep my promises and my girlfriend, my wife, always gets what she wants. And I am happy and

proud to be the one that gives it to her. In every end there's a new beginning. Learning to cope with struggles, pains, and hardship's only lets us
appreciate the good times that much more, and it also makes us strong.
May I bring forth the knowing within...

SHADOW'S OF HOMOSASSA

◆

am an eye witness and a resident to this well-known area that whatever it is that lives in those woods whether it be a skunk ape or a man in ghuillie suit, something lurks in those woods. While many people are unaware they are being spied on by something, I was aware of it. I believe it spies on people mostly at night time when it feels safest to sneak around behind trees and bushes and what have you. I don't know if its cops, a man in a suit, or a real live skunk ape either way it makes for a hell of a story. I personally can't fathom any man wasting his time like that even if he was paid by the cops it just seemed to be to unrealistic of an idea. After seeing what I saw that night it has had me thinking about what exactly it was for some time now. To the point where I almost hadn't mentioned it to anyone or talked about it at all out of fear of people thinking I was bat shit crazy. This story would not be the first account of something creepy going on in the background of this area. I can tell the difference between a delusion in the woods during the day and at night time, compared to an actual real shadow in the light of the night. A neighbor's back porch light was what caught this monster poking his body out from behind a live oak tree. It gives me chills as I think about it while writing it out. What in the hell was it? Really??? I had the thought of jumping the fence and running over there and holding it up, but didn't, out of fear of not coming back over the fence. I asked Riggs if he had seen what I just saw and he shook his head "no." I was thinking "gypsie!," I needed him to see it to.

Every once and awhile there seems to be a victim. Like the body Leland found near Mason Creek. It was no secret something was out there, especially after Stephen's death.

There are screech owls and the larger night owls, who send out mating calls and calls of the wild "screeeeeech-screeeeeech," and "hooooooo-hoooooo," in which I feel are my protection against any evil spirit, skunk ape, or monster, whatever it may be is not of afraid to kill. I find dead animals that it hunts down from time to time. Like birds, raccoons, squirrels, and other big rodents. The cops thought when they found Stephen dead in the neighbor's backyard that it may have been an overdose until they realized he had been beaten by something in the back of his head. It's something much deeper. Like the song, "he was only 17 but the river runs deep." I believe in animals as being spiritual creatures like ourselves. They have a soul and I believe they look out for us good people, and can travel along pathways to other dimensions if they want, or even be used by the spiritual God's of the universe as vessels to oversee and protect us from evil and who knows what else. I thank the Spirit Gods daily because without them our good would not prevail. They like it when someone believes in them and will stand with them without physically seeing them. We live by faith not by sight.

Now one night I was hanging out in my friend's backyard. I noticed a ghost light shining on over the fence in the neighbor's behind a live oak. I was staring into the neighbor's light and tree for about a good thirty seconds when out of nowhere a creature stepped out from behind the live oak tree and looked dead at me. It sent chills up my spine. I was shell shocked and couldn't quite gather what it was that I just saw, all I know is that it was built like a man but moved like an animal. It's about midnight. 12:00 AM late in the morning time if ya'll know what I mean. Coo coo time... I was startled but didn't say anything just looked on as he stared at me and then crawled and creeped back behind the large oak tree, and back out of sight. "What was that?!" is what my mind said to myself without saying anything like I was bat shit crazy but I knew what I had just saw was something real that people on tv only dream about seeing in real life. Had my friends and I conjured up a real live skunk ape? Simply by quietly partying at night time in the backyard. Not to quietly though or else he wouldn't have heard us.

He was tall and skinny with moss hanging from his head, shoulders, and arms. He had been spying on us all night I presume and of course I was the only one who saw him and I was way too scared to chase him down even though my gut really wanted to my heart wasn't ready to take that chance even though I felt like my mind could have taken him one on one hand to hand in that moment. But who knows what the outcome would have been if I did....

I always knew something lived back in those woods whether it be some sort of ape or a man with too much time on his hands its real and something or someone is living out there in those woods and comes closer at night time when it's safer. Creepiest thing I ever saw in my entire life. Beware and keep your wits about you in the woods at night time because you never know what could be out there. I do know it likes to kill whatever it is. He is sneaky whatever it is. Stephen was found dead with bruises to the back of his head like something beat him with a rock. There are long trails for them to travel north and south and on up into Georgia and Alabama. They can come and go that way. The skunk ape or big foot is not really scared of us humans I think and it sees us as easy targets but only attacks when the time is right and plans very carefully... Anything that can catch a bird or squirrel is somewhat of a skilled hunter especially if its primitive.

You will only see him if he wants you to be seen and why he would let me see him that night is somewhat of a mystery to me as well. I have thought about trying to look for him again one day. I must be careful whatever I do because the skunk ape is very dangerous creature and smart when its full grown and matured. It is not scared of us, yet we should be scared of the ape, no doubt in my mind. It deserves our respect.

ABEL IS WILLING

O nce upon a time in heaven, long ago, lived a boy named Abel. He was the chosen son of Jesus and only wanted to make him proud. He was very well known and respected for his great sacrifice and offering of the great lamb for Lord Jesus. Jesus was pleased. Yet some became bitter and jealous of him. Since Abel knew how to ask for guidance, he made a mighty offering. In which Jesus was pleased. Abel sought help and guidance from a king nearby to who he was a servant too. Abel was always very loyal and happy to serve. After consulting with a nearby King they both had agreed that a blood sacrifice would be what catches the Lord's choice, and it did. For Jesus had been pleased. Abel, the Sheppard, chose the best lamb out of his herd to offer our Lord. It was a very manly and bold offering he thought but he knew it would work.

In heaven he was well respected, yet some were jealous because of how lucky he had been. It was a small town at the time, and a small tribe of people ranging from 2,000 to 2,500 people. He had a wooden boat with oars to entertain himself during the day. Every morning after washing the dishes, Abel would row his boat out into the cove and float with the giant sperm whales. He had a great sense of peace and happiness here in the water. The whales were his friend's and he was not afraid to swim with them. It was like he had a divine connection with these whales. Not once did he ever worry about them flipping the boat or hurting him because they were docile like gentle giants floating beside him. Sometimes his good friend Noah would accompany him. They both feared the Lord our father, though they were his family, and Abel was the one who always found the courage to speak up for them and his entourage in times of discipline.

Abel also had a tree house in heaven. It was a simpler time then and the tree house was equipped with tin cans for phones with line attached to them for communication between him and his friends. They worked outstandingly, and you could feel the vibrations when speaking into the cans. The tree house had a window to look out of and was set back on the edge of the town near the forest over-looking the small village. The days were long and hot in the summer before they left out and the sun was always bright while Abel spent time playing sometimes all day in his tree house in the shade.

At home by the beach Abel would do his dishes in the afternoon by hand and day-dream of times before when there was more technology like dishwashers, cars, and computers. He felt he couldn't wait to get to listen to his favorite guided meditations. It was what he looked forward to in the future on earth and in heaven. Everyone knew there would be a time when most of us here would journey to earth on a Godly mission to help the world. Abels decision.

He thought to himself I was always good at typing, with a smile on his face. This boy was very special and was believed to be the one that came from an even higher place then this one in what was expected to be heaven. For what goes down can also have gone up. Abel believed in never leaving a man behind and that is what he based his decision upon even though many people did not agree with the boy he felt it was the right thing to do before going higher, plus he had an unshakeable faith in his GOD and the angels he would attract in the magical forest. He has GOD inside of him. In memory as well a whole page in the book of magic is dedicated to the boy. He was living proof of a perfect and pure heart. A very intuitive boy, he always had great ideas for the future alongside a few of the other elders. In which he had much love and respect for the ones he looked up too. They made him proud.

After the day-dream and dishes were done he would go forth into the center of the small village following by his father Jesus' side. Jesus would speak to him words of wisdom and Abel would listen and always re-buddle with good intuitive questions. Jesus would talk and Abel listened carefully. In the village it was like a city where most of the people resided during the day. Jesus would point out different things about the village and Abel always wondered about the town derelicts that always looked so poor. Abel wondered why and just felt compassion towards them. He just wanted to help them. He witnessed them doing some sort of powder they had either made or found themselves. Out of curiosity Abel always liked the idea of a good party and even having a weed smoke. He could remember the one time he smoked with Merlin the towns wizard out of a long, long, pipe widdled from wood in the forest with some other friends, he felt so free and so high, he was so happy that day.

Planet Earth had been calling and praying for help for some time now and many people were looking forward to going but heaven was waiting for the right moment to go and send the help to everyone that they needed. It wasn't until Abel was old and mature enough. Then he was ready to answer the prayers and Jesus said yes. Abel really did not want to leave this higher place in heaven for he was happy with his father and heavens simplicity long ago. Everyone else was eagerly waiting to go because they felt bored and ready for some action. Deep down Abel was scared because he knew the quest, he was on would not always be easy for him. Jesus never wanted us to forget where we came from and why he kept things simple.

Abel was excited to try some new things but stored a great deal of fear as well. Like the rest of the people. Abel also knew he had a job to do and foresaw that it wouldn't always be all that easy for him. It was a major sacrifice on his part for his girlfriends were there in heaven with him. He would miss them and could only hope that God would let them meet once again on Earth as well. Due to the fact we all were re-born.

Trusting God and his higher power a whole page is dedicated to Abel in the book of magic and was considered a true genius. Abel is a beautiful soul, a young man, and so he packed his small bag, tied it to a stick and prepared himself for the long journey down out of heaven to earth through the forest and on out the gates of the village and into the galaxy. The gateway between the two worlds.

I also forgot to mention there was another special girl like him who was very jealous of Abel and his brother for they were so lucky to who they are. She was constantly trying to stir up trouble and challenge their intelligence. Through the forest it became quite a nuisance to the two brothers while traveling. She followed them the whole way and wouldn't let them get away easily. It seemed as if it was her job to do her best to make Abel's life a living hell due to her sly jealousy of the boy.

On the way to Earth, when they were leaving heaven Abel was worried of the people with guns on earth. Walking next to Jesus he re-assured Abel not to worry of their guns for the power he beseeched is far greater than anything they could even imagine. Abel was then blessed by his father with the power of invisible fluid energy. To thine own self be true, Abel thought. The most powerful gift the one could receive. The energy and light force of the universe that we all need. Something for his protection... Abel knew this.

So with his clothes on a stick, they were off through the woods. The angels followed Abel and have been by his side the whole time and even to this day. Nelachael, his guardian that he named himself. Abel loved him so much. He was Eternally grateful.

After a forgettable journey the small group of angel people made it to the moon from heaven. This was the jumping off point. Quite a spiritual power they possessed. This was the point of no return, one to go down in the record books. They all had to take a leap of faith, all of them, by being reborn and having to trust the holy spirit would remember for them. And so it came to pass. Thy kingdom came. For Abel now had to be re born in order to go into the world, a command from his higher power, the true oracle, the only real oracle in the universe. Its magnamity is so great, you will shun yourself. A command from his higher power. Abel listened and Abel trusted, Abel is worthy.

He had a purpose for being there and after affixing all his plans he flew off the moon like stardust into his chosen mother's womb. Like any angel. Then stitched by God himself to fit in with the people on earth, and to be himself, a lot like superman. Moral of the story he saved a womans life one time.

His destiny had already been written before him and his plan came true but not without some hiccups. It unfolds perfectly in the end through our God and the father and the son and the holy spirit. With God in the heart of Abel the one who answered the world's prayers. Throughout his lifetime on Earth, he gave a solution to the broken and afflicted and addicted throughout time. He gave faith to the faithless. He gave money to the selfish. He gave people that deserved to be punished, well he gave them serenity; and free will to all. He gave the weak and helpless, protection and by himself he gave the whole world enlightenment just as his father had given him. The story of a young man named Abel who selflessly placed himself behind others and giving hope and answers from above. Amen. The End...

To be continued.

A DRAGON TELLS A TALE
WITHOUT A TAIL

T here was a man and then snap! There was a dragon snake driving a pontiac, built from a chevrolet, smoking marijuana out of the holes in his skulls. Why you ask? Skulls is plural. Because he's an 8 headed dragon manifesting straight from his lair. As big as a persons magnificent magnamity high on PCP. Otherwise his ego. NO. His alter-ego. In which hes never tried PCP before and this is his first time.

Remember the want to be cadillac I mentioned before, with the headliner peeling off the roof? Well its late at night and the ride was feeling a lot like a roller coaster. He begins to really start tripping right now. Screaming and yelling out the window hauling ass down the street and around turns. When all of a sudden a black cat runs out into the road crossing his path. Now he could look at this two ways. Is it a sign? One being the old wives tale but that this cat had no tail. Which is bad luck. Or because the cat had not had a tail that in turn it really actually is great luck. But what he chooses next in the car will be the journey of a lifetime. Kind of like a turtle having to walk a mile and he's hungry, angry, lonely and tired.

Did I mention thristy too. So hot and bothered he chose to make it a good ending by not caring what people thought about his now imaginary dragons tail that was no longer missing. Quite uncomfortable having a tail while driving he thought. That cat has to be great luck like halloween on friday the 13th and Jack Dawson winning a hand of poker before the titanic sets sail. Winner, Winner, chicken dinner. So I stopped at the jiffy and bought a scratch off and a cow tail. That cat will be my best friend whose a bigger fiend then me one day.

So like the poker game before the titanic set sail the dragon snake wins the poker game he was playing in his head while driving a pontiac marijuana, I mean chevrolet to a ball room in the UK and shades on at night over the Atlantic Ocean from America on a rainbow bridge he had never seen before. No he didn't need any gas.

Now everyone is dressed to the nines in the UK. Already he nearly gets in a fight and notices somethings not right when up to his sight blinded by the light of her beauty, he rest assured then everything will be alright.

Than he lost his thought like the girl in the Hootie and the Blowfish song, TIMEEEEEEEEEEE will tell a perfect story. Having faith while playing truth or dare like the light in the dark and a ying yang twin. Add an A and that's Twains handwriting on the paper that day Tesla's genius light came on. The one he didn't think he posessed for all those years.

Running down a hallway for dear life because the trip had become to much like a hurricane in florida's most southern point in his head. He finds himself alone with the door closed but not remembering how he got there in some room inside the palace in the UK.

Quietly out of the darkness came a dragon Queen with black lingerire and black leather straps. She was sexy as a female homosapien, but with a tail. At least that's what his eyes were seeing after all the PCP in the car on the magic carpet ride there.

Reaching for the balls and grabbing them from behind she had him in her clutches for the first time in a long time and even the caged birds were now chirping inside the master bedroom. The scent of a woman had him so aroused he could have built a city with that erection. Feeling like he wants to cum already he knows the drugs are the reason for that.

While he was holding it back she put a black head band over his eyes and proceeded to be a tease. Like a female cat. Lord knows the sin of this woman and is forgivable for just how erotic the sensation of her touch is. Something every man must know.

With the fire blazing high and hotter then before you could really feel the intensity of this special moment for her. The dragon snake man had no idea, as if he was a blonde on main street. It had been so long he had forgotten all about the time when he thought he knew her. She whispered in his ear from behind squeezing tighter. "Got ya now right there Mr. Big shot." "I always told ya it'd be love forever!" It's a goose.

As time went on the suspense grew thicker between the two. A pause and a long silence and after a moment or so, a twist like this, and he was on top of her on the couch by the fire. That's exactly what she wanted and with a growl he tore off the head band and saw the woman of his dreams come back for him amidst a snow storm in hell.

All in his mind while hes driving a pontiac made from a chevrolet he suddenly transforms back into his former self a handsome, stunning, and strapping gent, and so does she, like Fiona and Shrek or when the princess kisses the frog. Now king and queen of there domain once again.

Moral of the story nothing lasts forever because when the dragon snake thought there was no going back to reality is when PCP slighted his journey home to a place he thought he'd never see. He had no idea like a blonde on main street, or just like the mystery of his own heart... They lived there happy ending. To be continued....

THE SNAKE BITE

O ne summer evening I went over to my good friend, Colon's house for a visit. The place where all the neighborhood kids go to hangout after school and pre-parties. Naturally we had plans to go to Tami Ami's, a local bar we all liked to drink at downtown. They had plenty of games for us, to keep us going on late nights. It was Colon, Nick, and I. We were all very good friends and tend to have a great time together at the bar's downtown. We met up with Aaron and a few other people that night around 10 p.m. We were already a little buzzed before we got there from pre-drinking at Colons house. Needless to think, it was going to be one of the get drunk kind of nights.

I stayed close to the bar and played basketball with Aaron who by the way is very sexy and damn good at the free throw basketball game that we both loved so much. Collin and Nick stayed busy on the pool table going back and forth winner to loser, and loser to winner. They both are very evenly matched so it's hard to call it.

Pretty much the same deal with Aaron and I playing the basketball free throw game she's very good for a girl so we were closely matched but in the end, I managed to win. She did beat me a few times though throughout the night. She was one of the girls apart of my clique that I kind of wished maybe I should have tried dating her more realistically, but because she had a kid with one of our close friends we never really played it out. For me it just seemed like out of respect I never fully put the moves on her except one time we ended up making out, in which I found out she was a very good kisser. One thing about my girlfriend is, she has got to be a good kisser, very important to me.

So as the night went on we all got drunker and drunker and the night kept getting funnier and funnier. By the end of the night we were all watching Pineapple Express by the bar. The good old days. I don't regret those nights with my friends, none what-so-ever. I really do miss those nights.

Now before it got too late and any of us got to drunk we decided to leave after the movie ended, it was about 1:30 in the morning. I had some goodies I had scored from a close friend so Collin, Nick, and I went back to Collin's house for a little after party and to bless the rest of our night. The car ride home was delicious, with the windows down, a nice cool summer night with the breeze oh so right we headed to the garage for a little weed session.

By the time we got home Justin, Collin's brother was there to greet us. We came around side to the backyard and could smell Justin's clove cigarette long before we made it back there. We knew it would be another nostalgic night if Justin was home, he was a very adventurous soul and you could never tell what he might be up to next. "Heyyyyy Justin, what's up brother man!" We all greeted Justin once we were all back there we talked for a while and figured out our game plan. We decided to take this party into the garage where we could be a little bit louder and smoke our pot without getting into any trouble. I had my bong stored back there which by the was very expensive glass on glass custom piece with a frog on it. We all loves that piece until it got knocked over and broken.

The whole time were getting lit Justin wouldn't shut up about this snake he caught earlier in the day. Like I said Justin was very adventurous and you could never tell what he might have in store for you at home. On this night, it was a Pigme Rattler snake. He had caught it out in the yard and managed to get it into one of his fish tanks without being bit. He had a long stick with two ends on it, that he would use to pin the snake down with, then slowly and carefully pick the snake up from behind his neck and head. Pigme rattlers are not very big snakes but very, very poisonous. All three of us are about drunk and stoned as can be as Justin is showing us this snake he caught. "Whoa, dude, that thing looks wicked!' We were all three quite amazed but as of no shock to Collin he was like here watch let me get him out for you guys to see him close-up. We were like, "no Collin it's okay you don't have to pick him up for us." Collin said, "no I want to," and with a quick snatch to the back of the snake's head Collin had a quick and pretty good grasp on the back of the snake's head and neck.

He was all black and only maybe about a 10-12 inches long. He had very big head with strong jaw muscles and razor-sharp teeth with venom so poisonous it can kill a horse. His fangs were small but you can tell by looking at them he was not a friendly snake. "Ohhhh whoa, alright Collin that's enough put him back before someone gets hurt.' "HAHA I know right!" As Collin went to go throw the snake back into the tank, where Justin had made a little home for him with moss, sticks, branches and dirt from the yard, the snake turned on Collins hand as he let him go into the tank, and like lightning, "whap!" The snake turned and bit Collin right between his thumb and index finger on his hand. Collin jumped back grabbing his hand and yelled, "OWWW!!!" "Did he get you?!" we asked...

Collin showed us his hand and right between his thumb and index finger there were two small little drops of blood coming from Collin's hand. "He must have gotten you if your bleeding..." "Yeah, but I'm not bleeding very bad so maybe he didn't get me that good..." "I don't know Collin those things are pretty poisonous..." By this time of the night we were all freaking out because it was late and we were so drunk I don't think we knew how to go to the hospital... We asked Justin the snake expert, "do we need to take him to the hospital or is he going to be okay?" Justin cleaned Collin's hand up and after looking at it very closely decided that the snake didn't get him that bad and that we would wait and see... Nick and I said "okay, I guess were going to get out of here now that that's over." Make sure to call us if something comes up... We both went home scared and worried about Collin.

That same morning, I got a call from Nick. "YOOO Collins in the hospital!" "What is he alright?" "No. I guess through the night he could barely sleep and was sweating and dehydrated. Before the sun could come up his hand was swollen and started turning black and blue.!" His father immediately rushed Collin to the hospital and got there just in time. The doctor said, "if you would have waited another hour you would have risked losing your whole hand from the venom." The doctors administered Collin the anti-venom and had to cut out a segment of dead tissue, in-order to stop the spread of the venom. Way to close of a call. We all felt bad because we should have thought to bring him to the hospital much sooner but we really didn't know any better.

The next time I saw Collin his hand was all wrapped up from the surgery, and now had a bad ass snake story to tell. He was lucky to have survived and not lost his finger or hand in the process. We all blamed Justin as a joke but there were no hard feelings. Needless to worry, Justin got rid of the pesky, old, pigme rattler snake before it could get out and do anymore damage to either one of us, or the cats that hang outside and in that old garage.

THE DEAD LADIES KITCHEN

From a young age I had always wanted to work for the family's termite and pest control company, and so I did. By the time I was ten years old I was working on the fumigation crew dragging sand bags, carrying tarp, and running hot seams. I was a hard worker and very dedicated to my job. I had high hopes of one day being the owner and taking over my father's position so I always worked extra hard to try and make that happen for myself.

As I matured, I climbed the family ladder for the business and eventually had the role of being a service technician and drove my own truck. At age sixteen I was running my own pest control route out of my own truck and enjoying it thoroughly. It was a very good and lucrative job for any teenager. I would go to school in the mornings and in the after-noon I was off to work. The money came fairly easy and life was good. I had many good stories by the time I was eighteen since I visited about an average of ten to fifteen houses per day all with different scenarios. In this line of business theres no telling what surprises the day might hold for you.

One surprise in particular came one scorching summer day. I was working for my father's friend Greg who managed an old assisted living facility way out in Seminole Florida. About a thirty-minute drive in the morning from our shop in St. Petersburg. I conducted the pest control service on every one of the retiree's apartments. Forty-two buildings and about a total of 375 apartments. Without being rude, I met a lot of different and very interesting older people from all over the world who come to retire in Florida, and one female in particular who was very loud and pushy and always wore to much make-up. I had to be on time for her or she would be sure to complain to the staff if I wasn't. Nobody that lived around her liked her and they would go out of there way to avoid this woman altogether. She also had a raspy voice from smoking so many cigarettes and smelled like an ash tray covered up with too much perfume.

One month I came to Heritage the apartment complex, to do the pest control just like I always had done. I went into Greg's office first thing in the morning to get the master key so I could make sure to spray al the apartments before the day was up. The day was going smoothly as usual without any problems, it was beautiful outside and everyone was in a good mood that morning. At least until I got to building number seventeen. It was quiet and nobody was around, it was just me, hard at work with the master key knocking on doors and going into spray if nobody answered.

As soon as I entered the hallway to the old apartments there was an awful smell lingering throughout the hallway. At first thought I figured it was someone cooking some food of ethnic origin since I had smelled nasty cooking food like this before. There were also huge black flies buzzing around in the smelly hallway entrance to the front doors of the apartments.

There are two floors an upstairs and a down. To make my job easier I always start from the top and work my way down. Immediately I jogged up the stairs through the stinking hall and up to the top apartment. I knocked on the door and nobody was around so I waited patiently for someone to answer the door. After several moments and waiting patiently when nobody came to the door, I figured no one was home and used my master key to get in so I could spray for bugs and leave my card.

I was literally spraying fly's right out of the air. I opened the door and a wave of disgustingly warm smelly air swept pass me, and as I looked down at the door frame to start spraying, there was a one-pound hamburger package of meat laying rotting on the floor. I thought, "well geez that must be where the awful smell is coming from." Although I would have been wrong because as I began to enter the living room, I looked up into the kitchen and there she was lying naked, dead on the kitchen floor completely black and blue from Rigor Mortis setting in.

I jumped up in the air with my pest control can in hand and screamed, "AHHHHHH! What in the hell!!!" I thought I had seen a ghost. I took a second look and had a second scream, "AHHHHH! It's real, she's real, and shes dead, gross!" "I think it's the lady that nobody likes who wears to much make-up!" I ran as fast as I could back to Greg's office with my pest control can in hand screaming and yelling the whole way, "Greg!!! Help! You're not going to believe this!" Finally reaching his office Greg smiling with a big smile say's, "What?!" He yelled back and I said "Greg there's a dead lady with too much make-up on in her kitchen back there, you have to come see!" Instantly Greg burst into laughter and thought it to be to damn funny. I was like "why are you laughing I'm freaking out over here!!" "Now whats going to happen?"

Greg already knew since he worked there it wasn't the first time someone croaked in their apartment without anyone knowing. I guess it happens all the time in a facility like this. She must have been there for at least a week rotting away. Nobody liked her so nobody ever checked on her. She was the mean, pushy lady with too much make-up.

I can look back and laugh today but at the time I was freaking out because I had never seen anything or smelled anything like it before in my entire life. Both Greg and the Cop who questioned me made fun of me the whole time while giving my statement. Greg was like, "you should have seen the look on your face when you came running back to my office! Classic!" We can both laugh our ass's off now since the whole story in all was just an insanely hilarious experience.

The old lady, nobody liked, who always wore to much make-up is how she was remembered. But hey props to her because she's now laughing in heaven since she got a story written about her. She made history by stroking out in her kitchen before dinner one day. I wonder if she chucked the chuck beef at the door trying to alert someone that she was dying while cooking dinner.

THE KEY, A PRAYER ANSWERED

I believe in the Bible and throughout my life I have had prayers answered but nothing quite like this. I guess you could say that I'm a little more spiritual then I am religious since I to am a sinner. I know God loves me and will not forsake me, even though my faith can get weak sometimes. There's a lot of truth to my spirituality and has taken me along time to understand what it really is. I once was given a key during one of my spiritual experiences and was able to bring it home with me. I remember having it made while I was in the spirit world. A skeleton key. Rare. Handmade. Priceless really.

Unfortunately for me at the time I was addicted to Meth which was a kind of spiritual lubrication for an experiment like this. Turns out. When my spirit made it back home to my body, out of desperation for my fix I traded the key for a tenth of dope. A priceless possession. Not before praying about it because I really did not want to lose this special key I had inherited from a close friend in the sky. I prayed, "God if this key is for me and its meant to be then let it be... Amen." I went on to trade my key for the dope that got me there in the first place, my home away from homes. I like to call it heaven.

Soon after that I left town, to get sober and sobriety I found. I worked very hard on myself and had a spiritual awakening that was to say the least very over-whelming. After a while I spiraled into a horrible depression and before I knew it, I was getting high again but now I see how it was apart of Gods plan, a plan bigger then my own. Now I was on a journey in finding my key and had no idea and was taken by surprise when I did. I was sober around two years before I re-lapsed, so it had been at least two longs years since I had seen my key and said that prayer.

One night I was at home stoned and tweaking by myself and feeling really good when a close friend of mine who reminds me of some good people in my life like Erica from high school. Sissy and Dizz had hit me up looking for some dope and things to trade with. They were like for sure come through. I had a little extra that night, so it didn't bother me to want to get out of the house and go play a trade with my good friends Sissy and Dizz.

I drove over there late that night around 2 a.m., and we were all three hanging out bull-shitting and making trades. I was having a really nice time getting to know Dizz whom I had never met before and it was cool.

Out of nowhere after being over there for about an hour or so some-body knocks on sissy's back door to her bedroom. It was one of Sissy's friend who I think may had been on the phone earlier with Sissy. She most definitely had the hots for me, and I felt the same, but being that we are still mature adults and wanted to see what she had been hiding we got past the sexual tension. She mentioned she had just been on a good trip with a friend. We all laughed about it and I still wonder today how long she had been holding on to this key that belonged to me.

As she commenced to break out the two old skeleton keys out of her bag, I thought, what could it be. One key looked evil and was like a dark old black prison gate key and the other key low and behold was my key in which was a much prettier in lay and had a cross in it. I always wanted to know more about that other key, but we have no idea where that one came from. All in a good night it was still two very cool looking keys, most definitely the big deal of the night.

I gasped for air since I hadn't seen my key in over two years. I quietly knew I had to do whatever it took to get my key back. A priceless possession my Celtic family key that had been especially made for me. It was a sign from above.

I could have kissed her! I didn't care, I was secretly in love with this woman, like she was somehow initiated by the one. She was most definitely a special girl in my eyes. Her and I crossing paths was most definitely by some sort of divine presentation. A prayer that was given to me. I had prayed and now two years later it came true. God works in mysterious ways sometimes.

Lucky for me we were all partying and wanting to get high together, so I had plenty to go around, plus I got my key back for practically nothing at all. We were all very happy after that. There I had it an answered prayer with physical evidence that the spiritual realm still exists. I know for a fact prayer works and I also have learned that God's timing is perfect. Here was a key that I had prayed for and given away and after two long years it made its way back to me, returning to its rightful heir. Almost like the key knew all along and had a mind of its own. I hope one day I can see exactly what door it opens for me. Once again all I know is that its pretty amazing and very real. I can still remember the night I received my key and know that it is a very precious story.

THE HAND OF FIRE

I came to in a dream standing in the middle of what looked to be an old European street paved with old bricks. The street was fit with town-home style architecture and construction about 2-3 story's high on each side of the road. There was a light breeze kicking paper trash around in the streets but quiet with nobody around. It was dark outside. Some of the street lights were flickering on and off and it felt quite empty like something had happened here and everyone had been evacuated. I was filled with a fear of impended doom.

As I began to walk, suddenly I felt something wanting to pull me back and down into a man hole in the middle of the street. Some sort of dark force, because nobody was here so it couldn't have been a person. I wanted to run and go knock on somebody's door for help but the more I tried running the more I was pulled down into the hole. I was eventually sucked all the way into the man hole after a few fighting moments. I was very scared and still asleep and could not wake up even though I wanted to… Isn't that the worst when your dreaming and you want to wake up out of a bad dream and you can't. Eventually I give in and wait till the dream is over or for a moment when I can wake up.

I gasped for air with a shocked stricken face and butterflies in my stomach. I was being pulled down and quite fast I might add. The light coming through the top of the man hole was getting smaller and smaller the deeper I was sucked down into the hole. I was being pulled down deeper and deeper by my ankles into complete and utter darkness. It seemed the only light there was left is radiating from inside myself and the little bit of light from the flickering lamp posts shining through the hole on the street up above, but was quickly diminishing, leaving me breathless and scared the deeper I sank. The moment I became completely hopeless and out of fight I thought "this is it. I'm going to die dreaming but at least it's not painful." At that same time, a huge hand made of red and orange flames came from high up above the street even.

The hand came all the way down out of the sky scooping me up out of the depths of darkness tossing me high up into the sky amongst the stars and clouds without burning me. Maybe that's how l lost my shirt. I suddenly grew long flowing, brown hair. Longer than I had ever had before. My shirt magically disappeared somehow but not my glasses, and was flying through the sky. I suppose my body wanted to feel the cool night air flying over it. I felt weightless and with arms spread like eagle's wings I was able to soar through the night sky back and forth flying amongst the stars and clouds for some time now.

Several moments had went by before I turned back into a boy and reality struck and gravity began to force me back down. I didn't free fall out of the sky I simply came fluttering down back and forth like a feather. I gently landed back down on the road with a running motion in which once I was firmly back on solid ground, I came to a quick halt.

Immediately gathering my thoughts and shaking off the shock, I ran to the first door I could find, on the right side of the street. Excited, and a little scared of what had just happened, I ran up to the steps and through the door with no expectations of anyone being inside, since earlier it was almost as if doomsday had approached and aliens or ghosts had sucked everyone down into the sewers. I was alone in this dream running inside and looking up feeling like I was soaking wet even though there had been no rain outside. Because of the pace I was running my body felt wet, it was like I was running fast inside to stay out of the rain perhaps. Dreams are funny like that. I was wet but there was no rain. I was soaking wet with water dripping off me from head to toe. All I'm wearing is a wet pair of jeans and a belt and glasses.

Up to my surprise my brother was hiding behind the dinner table crouched over with a small staff and his cloak on over his head and shoulders. The dream was suddenly turning into some Harry Potter spin off. All because of my brother Kevin, and his invisibility cloak in which I could still see him. He looked something like Quasimoto from Frankenstein the way he was crouched over. By my surprise his hair was now longer and wet too, but Lord knows there was no rain, and yet we both weren't moving so much as to be sweating that bad. I thought maybe he had an invisibility cloak to protect us from any demon or aliens. Thank God for the hand of fire. Ah yes, he did have an invisibility cloak. It was just because I am his brother that I could see him, we are connected and one with GOD.

I wanted to cry because I love him more than he knows and am glad he was there. If there was anyone I would want to make a last stand against demons, it would be with him. We are different but connected on a deep intellectual level. I wanted to tell him what I had just experienced, but before I could he put his one finger over his lips and said, "shhhhhh-hhhh." In the same way Mom would have done. Still nobody but us two inside this house, but not to mention, this was not our house. Kevin said quietly "follow me," and began creeping slowly out of the dining room and into the living room just passed the kitchen to our right. He crept pass me slowly crouched over heading towards the living room. I let him pass and as I'm following close behind I thought right than about bursting into laughter. It was then I woke up still in bed but completely able to remember the entire dream. Nothing seemed funny until I felt safe.

I can remember my dreams but I don't always remember enough of them to write with. Where with this dream I vividly remembered the entire dream, in which I had only had this dream one time. I was hoping to see what the escape route was going to turn into or if something was going to jump out at us like a demon, alien, or a zombie but unfortunately my own laughter wanted to wake me up beforehand. I thought about making up something to add to the ending of the dream, but instead, I kept it true and real as was exactly from the dream. After all that I had experienced in the end, all I could do was laugh. It was like a Heavenly father, Harry Potter, Walking Dead trio of a dream!

THE GOOD, THE BAD, THE UGLY

M y birthday is coming up soon. It's June now, beginning of summer
and Independence day is coming up so the town has been very active. Fireworks and lots of kids in the streets. The best times. I have
been clean for two years now and things were going pretty good except,
I was walking through hell and didn't even know it, and afraid to admit
it. Like my own prison. Even in sobriety like living the dream. Déjà vu
and reconciliations daily and just not knowing what the hell is going on.
I have a built-in forgetter and can choose to let go of whatever, whenever,
if things get to be too stressful. After years of not remembering when my
whole life came true and began being real I was shocked. Overwhelmed
to say the least. You never truly want to lose whose one-self is no matter
what the circumstances, especially if you are already an important person.
Life is deep. Live Bold and fiercely in who you are and what you are and
don't ever stop learning and seeking yourself. The spirit is real.

I can hear him speak sometimes, like that still small voice in the front
of your head. My guardian angel I gave him his name. I named him about
ten years ago when I was drunk one night. His name is Nelchael and he
is beauty, light, and love. Mine own spirit and I am his. I trust and love

him under God. For he is great and very real. Compassion runs deep in my family, and is in some ways indescribably cool, and beautiful. I might write a book about compassion, what it is, how it works, and why we use I and also why animals use it.

Now moving from the light and into the darker spiritual realm; like the demons, ghosts, and noises you might here from time to time usually at night.

I have seen and heard some real occurrences and conjuring's. I hear claps and something throwing rocks at my window. It could be myself but I'm not sure what he's trying to get me to do unless he's just playing with me. For example, when fear knocks or throws rocks and faith answered nobody was there. I tend to believe in the brighter side of things and I believe in more than just what we see. Some call it blind faith. Eventually God will reveal himself to you and keep the faith. Almost like old folk lore coming true, it's scary, and mind blowing, but just as I originally thought during my pledge, very cool, and nothing to be afraid of yet there is some truth to it.

Walking in my pledge was like walking through hell. A frozen time warp where you are constantly experiencing a sense of déjà vu, day in and day out even in sobriety. Like hein-sight is 20/20. With no end in sight and always hoping tomorrow will be different or better and it's not so, I am constantly singing the serenity prayer, just so I don't shoot myself kind of day. My head and my heart had become heavy laden yet my burdens were not real although I thought they were.

I never knew of the beast inside me until this year. It had reared it's ugly head for the first time in my life when I was half asleep one night at home. I wasn't sleeping good at all due to post-acute withdrawal symptoms from coming off from certain other drugs. It reminded me of Dr. Evil from the book Harry Potter because we're not supposed to mention it's name. I know God can in Jesus name help me through the pain and the struggles of living life in this world. I am a child of God not to be forsaken. I am not a bad omen. Demons are very unexpected thing. I just didn't want it in me. Like a bad dream it scared me.

When I had my flash-back I saw my white light glowing around the left half of my face and head. A true miracle walking because mind you I was clean for two years at the time. I know it was real and that I wasn't seeing nothing but the truth in the mirror. The other half of my face was a dark blue color and mind you had no shine. Nothing but a scared confused lazy eye but whatever or whoever it was seemed to be obedient and honorable. What does the blue and no shine represent or what does it mean. It's afraid of the light. It was as if I had been fighting with the good and bad that lived inside of me. My good shall always prevail, gracefully, honorably, most definitely and respectably. No worries. They can be drawn out with certain crystals and ancient reiki healing techniques. Then let go into space where the universe gets rid and knows what to do with them. Kind of like ghost busters. The Devil may try it but God stops it. One cool thing about spirits and demons is that I don't know if we will ever know exactly how they work.

No worries the universe knows what to do with evil spirits. I never knew drugs like that could be quite like that. Evil the Devil I was hoping wasn't going to be a factor in my life. I am now learning to take the good with the bad. Acceptance is the key to my problems and embracing all of life as I know it, is the best way for me to live. And a lot of people agree. I have heard an old shaman tell me once about the spirit of drug. An evil one maybe but there is a lot of good to be found there to. Love conquers all. Needless to think I try and see the best in all situations.

THE INVISIBLE BING AND TIME CRUSADES

$\blacklozenge$

So where to start. I'm going to be honest. I was on a six-month meth binge and during my journey a lot had happened to me spiritually and very unexpectedly. This is a true story and I survived it. I was chosen to do so and didn't realize at the time but was all a part of Gods plan for my life. I was doubted although I knew I am strong.

At some point in my journey my heart had been bugged. I had a spirit guide named Leland whom became my best friend at the time. He has a son named Isaac who was quite adorable. They were my best friends and my go to pal through this escapade. Fast forwarding to get to the moral of the story, along the way I found I had been burning the candle on both ends for quite some time through-out my life God made this possible because of my own reasons, fears, and doubts. I had been third eye blind but was always listening and taking direction at pivotal points in my life and today still am today. I know my spirit is real.

Now towards the end I was instructed by my spirit guide Leland to go to my future house where future me will be laying loosely resting, but not quite asleep, just exhausted from his journey through recovery to get to that point and the show he couldn't hold onto anymore. I brought my tool and was instructed to remove the plate with screws and remove whatever worm was inside his back-left shoulder. Right where the human heart is. I did so and removed a centipede like worm about six inches long quickly. I was a little disgusted and mad because this is me. Like I said I had reasons fears and doubts but no regrets. Rightfully so says I.

I used my magic I was provided to wave my hand over his shoulder and close and heal his back up in one easy swipe. I'm glad I got to see it myself. I knew that I loved him. He could not see me but knew that I was there hence I had to undergo the same process. God works in mysterious ways sometimes and does what it takes is necessary for himself and others. I worked as the invisible man or spirit so to speak that evening. I Came and went through the back door and as I left the screws in the garage I threw the bug in the pool for him to see the next day. Needless to think I went home and found myself alive in bed the next morning relaxed and renewed.

I went out back that morning and saw the big bug lying in the pool. As soon as I saw it I connected the dots right away. Had hopes of it not being true but knew how to handle this with acceptance. I fished the bug out of the pool smashed it with my boot and threw in the fire pit. I have a pool enclosure with no holes or tears for something like that to come through. The bug was pulled out of me and thrown in the pool on purpose for me to see. I told Leland the next day that I threw it in the pool and he asked why? In a sort of confused manor like I shouldn't have. I said because I want him to know for sure and see for himself. I know myself well enough to know that I thrive on the truth and wouldn't want anything less than that.

I had forgot who I was for a long time but kept the faith. I am favored by the lighter side of things in heaven due to my good nature. So I survived to fill the will of God in heaven here on earth. I was given the power to get rid of it so I did. I could not see my spirit that night but intuitively felt and knew his presence.

I was almost a year sober on that day not realizing that when I left I was basically coming home to the same day in which I had left. Acceptance was the answer. I had proof love is also acceptance. It may not be something we feel all the time but I sure do try and feel it as much as I can. In being clean I have been proving to myself that I can make love last. I can also create love myself at any given moment in my life if I allow myself to do so. I simply allow it to be part of my nature and let it flow in and out and around me all day. Lustful ways don't last and were simply not worth it because I am human. Perhaps if I wasn't human lust might have been the best drug. Today I can be high on life, love, and legacy.

I don't ever want to live like that again and sometimes wish it weren't true. I struggle with being grateful for it but I do find gratitude when I realize how much I have grown and learned about myself through such horrifying struggles. A lot was given and taken and sacrifices were made. My fear, doubt and pain are revealed and relieved at the same time facing it all with real clarity and knowing that this is just a-part of who I am today.

THE BARN FIRE

ong ago in Ireland during the Celtic age, lived two friends who were always supportive of one another. They watched one another's back like two friends are supposed to do. Since the one-man James was like a Celtic philosopher himself, his friend Justin would follow him everywhere and transcribe for him the amazing things that would spring from his lips at times of inspiration. It was a school graduation and James found himself at the top of his class. It was a day of celebration for everyone that weekend.

Later that night and in the evening James and Justin gathered like two friends will do. They started drinking it up inside the barn as the day began to die down and all the other towns people went to sleep. Or so that is what they thought....

It was around 9:30 pm that night when everything went wrong so quickly neither of them knew what to do.

It was a two-story red wooden barn with a flight of steps going up into the loft. There were hail bails and loose hay everywhere stuffed into each corner of the barn. That night it was now completely dark outside so there were several candles lit to keep up the light for our eyes. Also, we had the wooden table which housed our scotch and brew...

They laughed and yelled all night talking back and forth to each other when suddenly Justins arms went up and he fell into the table where the candle was lit. All the hay laying everywhere all over the barn went up into flames very quickly. Little did James know dharma would be on his side the whole time.

Before James could even react to putting out the flames, he had to save his friends' life first. In his mind, that is what made sense. James really did care. He was considered a caregiver like none other. Where no good deed ever goes unpunished.

Justin had rolled a meter or two away into the side of the barn close to where the fire was. It got smokey fast in the enclosed barn was heating up quickly.

James quickly checked on his friend, grabbed him up and threw him over his shoulder as fast as possible. Now James was a big and hefty man back then and was always admired for his big muscles and working abilities. Not to mention that magic he possessed. The miracles they witnessed always astonished them.

Respectfully James walked out of the barn with Justin is his arms safely. By the time he had secured Justin and ran back into the barn to put the fire out the whole barn had gone up in flames. What a pickle they were in.

Suddenly before the towns people showed up, James had no water to put out the fire. James could not put out the fires and the whole barn burnt down, down to the ground. The towns people were now becoming aware of the situation and come rushing to make sure everything and everyone was okay, but everything was not okay. The initial fire set off a chain reaction of fires and about 6 more houses were burnt to the ground down the tree line by the lake. Nobody was hurt, just startled.

Once outside James say in wonder, jaws open, and eyes open wide while he watched the barn completely go down in flames. Slowly as Justin re-gained his own consciousness the towns pilgrims had come running to help and see what had happened.

At first the towns people in Ireland were terribly upset and angry blaming James for everything and pointing fingers his way. Because not only did the barn burnt down, but 6 more houses alongside the lake had been burnt down too. All the people made it safely out from their homes before the fire and smoke could harm them. Nobody died or got hurt it was a miracle everyone was safe. What is worse is one of the girls who lived in one of the houses had been terribly upset with James. All her savings were locked up inside the house as it all went up into flames and all her money was lost in the fire. Her savings were for her schooling when summer ends and the new year begins. She was livid and very adamant about blaming James for everything. At first it looked as if they were going to lock the two of them up for all the ruin and chaos caused!

James pleaded his case and shortly after his older sister, Mary, showed up in his defense right there on the spot. She was an elder among the community, well respected, and considered one of the higher ups in the village. James was lucky, as if dharma were on his side that night, if not for Mary, James would have been taken away and worse.

The towns people were in an up-roar blaming James for not putting the fire out first. James did not know what to do all he could think was right would be to save himself and his friend. He had no idea other houses would be burnt to the ground as well. He did what he thought was right and best. He had no ill-intentions on anything bad happening that night. It was an accident. This was the basis he was let off on, after Mary explained for him that it was not his fault but an accident. James was under one condition that he would re-construct new houses for the villagers and pay the young girl back her lost money. James agreed and was let go to help clean up the town.

Justin was so thankful for his friend James and would do anything to re-pay him like a loyal friend would. James never was too concerned if he had Justin as a friend, he would be okay.

The town commenced to re-build the new houses with James by their side helping them every bit of the way. It was hard working summer for James but he managed to get it all done by the next summer. He had then redeemed himself and was hailed high once again for paying back the young girls money. All along James was so grateful for his beautiful sister Mary. If it were not for her defending him, they would not have listened to James' word alone. He would have been jailed or worse lost his head. Had he not had Mary's protection from the people that would be exactly what would have happened. James did the right thing the noble thing and was awarded handsome like. He got to keep his life!

Moral of the story sometimes we take what little life in time we have for granted and the caring people around us. Even though it had been over-looked because of the tragedy James was honest, had good intentions, and he cared enough to save another man's life once again before the barn burnt down, down into ashes.

That to me is enough grounds for a man to be forgiven for not putting out the fire first. Everything was going so well for the village and when that happened it was heart breaking to a lot of people but accidents do happen and Justin and James were brave and re-built the village so it was even nicer than before! God works in all our lives in such Suttle, mysterious, a miraculous way that sometimes we do not understand why or how dreadful things happen, but if you notice after every death there is re-birth into a newer better and even more spectacular life that you could ever imagine before.

In the Celtic era magic was deemed crazy and few people knew about it and practiced it in privacy. Magic was unknown. Today God's magic is being noticed increasingly everyday by everyone. Like the miracle of being selfless enough to save one's life. Then re-building a town into a nice neighborhood by the lake. James was clapped for and hailed highly. The young girl was then again proud and honored to know James for all that he had done that year! James had paid her back all the money in full... Amen.

ROCK BOTTOM

f you would have asked me as a child that my life would have turned out the way it did I would have probably got most of it correct except for the lack of financial freedom in my life. Although I am better off than some people I struggle to keep a roof over my head from time to time. Some call it the lonely road of faith and to me that describes my adulthood life quite well.

One morning after a long deep sleep I was woken up by a phone call from my girlfriend whose name I would rather not mention out of respect. Oh and before I go any further this story is the fundamental reason of why we all have freedom of speech protected by our constitution and our founding fathers. To me this is a true story but to others it may just be another tall tale or false testimony.

I got the call, woke up and went out to old town to meet her like she had asked. I got my fix and we were off to the park as far as I was concerned it was just another day. Funny thing was I usually always drive but this day she had her own car for us to ride in but hey I don't complain when it comes to get free dope for hanging out. I would be a perfect person I believe if it wasn't for my addiction problems and that's okay because im not even close to being the only one.

We arrived at the park and got out of the car to see what all the commotion was about. All she told me was there was something I needed to see. Now this past life seems to me to be nothing but a dream and vague experience. As we got closer to the center of the park where everyone was heading there was the spirit of JESUS with arms wide open on the left and a burning ring of fire on the right. I know it sounds crazy but after having had a spiritual awakening this was just another one of the many memories I had from past spiritual experiences. Now me a God fearing man who is high on dope and a low self esteem was well ready to run left into heaven where I know I belong. But she wanted to go to hell in a hand bag I suppose since she prompted me to stay right. My whole life flashes before my eyes and it was almost like I already knew all the answers and this seemed to me to be the right thing to do anyways to perhaps pay my own karmic debt and then some. Get right with God and self first on earth before going home for good. I tend to be really hard on myself sometimes even when I know I deserve nothing but the best. Tricks are for kids silly rabbit but deep dowm I always knew what I was doing was the right thing no matter how bad others might hate me for it. So I took the trip and fell down into the burning ring of fire. I wemt down down down and the flames went higher.

I finally knew what it was johnny cash was talking about in his song from a hundred years ago. It was like being stuck in a bad dream like a nightmare that you cant quite wake up out of. A vision of what the bottomless pit off hell and boiling blood looks like. I often wondered afterwards if other who have seen the final stage of hell if its like the same for everyone or different... Leland a good friend of mine great even like Stephen. Or maybe in this moment my spirit guide like I have seen him before in other spiritual experiences when rapping I'm not afraid. I love that kid because without him being there I may have died or been trapped for good. The journey back up it gets better. Something like nine levels. But first I have to figure out how to get out of this hell hole of boiling blood and stinch that thanks be to GOD I could not smell. Without Leland being there it could have taken me along time to get out alone if at all.

It was like being trapped in the center of the earth with boiling blood instead of lava. I'm stuck standing on a small round stone like island staring at this pool of boiling blood as the ground and walls begin to shake and slowly but surely rising up from the pool of blood a great big monster on top of a large rock began rising out of the depths of the hot boiling blood. The best way I can describe the Devil himself was that he looked like Bowser from the Nintendo game Mario Kart. Maybe just the figment on my own imagination of what the devil looks like but to be completely honest I had never had thoughts like this before in my entire life. The thought of boiling blood when she said it was totally new for me. Not to mention the tiny little round cave with no exits in sight sound or feel. Just complete blackening quicksand when you try and fly out the further you get pulled down. My spirit knows how to fly so it was definitely one of my first escape tactics that quickly had to give up on because flying away didn't work here it only made it more difficult to get out.

So next I slowly climb to the top of the cave with no exits in sight hoping for the best. Up in the roof of the cave in the corner there's an attic access that you can't get out of. I stayed stuck in the portion of the attic for some-time struggling to find a way out or through it but failing miserably. No matter what I did I seemed stuck in this corner of an attic. I was ready to give up and throw in my towel and go to sleep right there when I remembered Leland!!! He was still hiding around somewhere. He had to be if not in my heart then where?... I hope and pray the best for him because he is a great friend. He might be pleasantly surprised if I ever hook him up with a truck load of money for him and Isaac. Together

Leland and I Peter Panned our way out of this evil sanctuary of disgust-ingness. It was as if we escaped through a tiny little poked hole in the darkness that brought us into the light and the next level up. I don't think I could take it down there for to much longer before I snapped into who knows what. May the knowledge of my life grow and manifest into my life. Receive this gift now and do exactly as she say's for a while. Amen.

The rest of the journey is a blurr but I remember when I see a picture or have a déjà vu. Like being the raccoon on the commercial. Some weird stuff you experience when walking through hell. I have never been into scary movies but they have grown on me a little bit.

I don't believe in coincidence and everything happens for a reason. Foxhole prayers are still prayers. We tend to forget until we need some-thing like a second wind or new life. Simply just being alive sometimes is satisfying enough. Like the feeling of not wanting or needing anything and being satisfied feels unusual. I don't really like it to be honest. I like the feeling I get from wanting or needing something.

I woke up the next day body back in my bed almost like it had never left. Luckily safe and sound back in purgatory which is the best place to be if living in hell. Leland and I spiritually made it through the night. Thanks be to God on this one for rights of passages and shadows on the sun. I went out for my morning weed session and the weather was amaz-ing even the birds were bumping. I found Leland outside his house in the yard that morning. He always likes it when I bring a little weed with me for the two of us especially on a morning after that. Before I could say anything to him he was like duuuuuddddeeeee.....! Why did you do that????! And I think I responded with the pledge that day like oh you must have forgot about that part. Because im a nincompoop remember. It was bound to happen that way especially when someone standing in my way. I was weak at the time and to nice for my own good, would let people take advantage of me a little too much instead of sticking up for myself just to avoid confrontation. Strong lessons to be learned of one self in experiences like these. Because of all that today I'm not such a push over and can do a little more than stand my ground if I have too. I also don't take such bad advice anymore.

DÉJÀ VU'

Have you ever had a sense of déjà vu everyday day in and day out for over a year? I have… Almost as if time had literally been frozen and I was living in the same day from 3 years ago every-day, nothing changed. Nothing was ever different. You would think it to be impossible. There had to be some math to it… Some sort of algarythm. The universe never seizes to amaze me. Nothing changes if nothing changes was the best answer I could get??? Not to mention I seemed to be the only person completely shocked by it. I understand we all see life differently but I would have expected more people to notice it. They may have been afraid. Like I was, but not too afraid to talk about what was going on in and around me. It was enough to drive me crazy.

Thank God for the power of prayer which seemed to be the answer and my saving grace. I continually asked God and myself what is this supposed to mean and more importantly when will it stop. Have I died and am living in some sort of dream warp like walking through hell with Johnny Depp. It always seems to be like living in the same day. Nothing changes if nothing changes. Everyone is on autopilot and just going through the motions except myself, a lot like Adam Sandler in the movie "Click." I even mentioned in a song I did, "I'm stuck in a time warp from 2004 though…" Not to mention the pain from being an ignorantly trusting person. Maybe it has everything to do with the drugs… Now there's a thought. Who would of thought. I always believed somethings are just too complicated to be possible. Yet it seems there's some stream of fluid motion that can make anything possible. Be the water. A glass of water is harmless yet it can save your life and replenish your body. On the other-hand it can be a tidal wave or hurricane and completely-demolish everything in its path. I was watching a martial arts movie and a young man was trying to prove himself worthy to fight in front of his master and when he tossed the glass of water at him the kid kicked the hell out of the water as hard as he could with excellent precision I might add. Master looked at him and said, "did you kick the water, or did you only think that you kicked the water."

I was given a will of passage. But it doesn't stop the spirits from conjuring at night and throwing stones at my widow. I hear a big pop from time to time and Moths the size of my hand that crop up out of nowhere. Ridiculousness. Something happened to me last night around 12 p.m. with Justin. We were smoking a joint and it's hard to describe exactly what it was like. Something had come over me in not such a good way because it felt so odd and strange whatever it was I think it was the spirit of the weed Gods. Thus Justin wouldn't shut up. He was talking too much and was quite irritating. It's like a competition with him. I think he feels threatened by me around girls. I don't like men that disrespect women. Makes me question our friendship.

I don't know where I was going with this story nor do I have a moral to it. I was just kind of seeing where it would go like some sort of freestyle writing. Anyways this is a true story of my life. Welcome to my world through my eyes. It's not always easy being me but it sure is great to be me from time to time. I'm a special person in someone's eyes and that's enough for me. Not sure exactly what the end of this story will look like to be honest. It hasn't been written yet so I still have no moral to it. Interesting because this story leaves with lots of questions and we all know how a smart person loves questions and has a thirst for knowledge in knowing things for a fact.

AN OUT OF BODY EXPERIENCE

W e all have what's called a silver that connects us to our spirit and the universe and it's actually a real thing and it works if you let it. Guided by a mediator into a sleep hypnosis I let my spirit get up out of my body a go fly away, all along keeping the idea of my silver cord connected until I am ready to return to my body. This has not been my first out of body experience but one that I remembered quite well and had most control over.

I came to in a domicile with about eight other people wearing life like a loose garment in what seemed to be a distant part or another part of the universe. We all were wearing these big round circular blue hats similar to the one Raiden wears in Mortal Kombat. It seemed everything was in a light blue like ora here. For some odd reason actor Jim Carey was there guiding our experience. We all looked up at one another and smiled. Then one by one we all started flying up exploring where we are and going on our own little adventures. I don't recall everything but I do remember flying, laughing and playing with my new found partner in the sky. We don't have wings yet are still able to fly by the energy of the spirit.

We landed on a blue beach shoreline together looking and laughing. Thinking how beautiful this place was we had never been before, well at least I hadn't she seems a little bit more familiar with this place then I was. Like she had been here before and was used to flying. The ora blue on this beach was more beautiful than anything I have ever seen before. Nobody else was there just the two of us so, we began to take advantage of our dream and the alone time and privacy of our minds, lost in the universe of the spirit world. We slowly began hugging and kissing and before ya know it we were making sweet love right there on the beach. It definitely got a little bit more intense as time went one but all in all was an amazing feeling and a great experience to say the least if you know what I mean.

In an out of body experience in most cases, you actually have control over your dream and do as you please as if you are actually there. It does take some practice and getting used to. We chose the doggy style position I suppose was the best for that moment on the blue beach. Not much thought went into it, it just happened that way. She was very beautiful to, like perfect. When it was over we both got up and she immediately kissed me on the lips and flew away. I also forgot to mention when your in a place of the spirit world you feel differently to like some sort of cool calm relaxing tantric like feeling. Almost like being on drugs without the drugs and better. I stood up took a look and a breath saw that I was still on the beach and decided to chill for a minute longer. Once I was alone on the beach long enough I asked to return to my body. I did enjoy the time alone on the beach after she had left. At first I was like no, but quickly I realized yes, as she did, and had my perfect moment alone of the beautiful blue beach after she flew away. The best way I can describe that moment alone is being like a moment of clarity like hmmmmm, I wonder how much better can it get? Probably not much, but who knows.

I was ready to get back to my body so down the silver cord I flew, back to my body lying in bed where I got to wake up with a beautiful brand new spiritual experience. You can refer to this as sleep hypnosis or out of body experience, spiritual experience, a controlled dream, and so forth. I looked at my clock and I thought I was gone for only about forty-five minutes but I had been asleep for about three hours. I could remember everything and had complete control over my experience, and it was a dream come true. I felt at total and complete peace with myself, a great feeling.

ALCHEMY

❖

I wrote a story one day at Dunkin Donuts. A dream I once had. I named the dream "Invisibility Cloak." Because it reminded me of Harry Potter. I was in the middle writing my story and everything was going smoothly. The weather outside couldn't have been better. I rode my bike up there to have coffee and to do some writing. Then out of nowhere a tropical storm hit the café. Huge dark clouds, pouring down rain, loud thunder and lightning. There seemed to me to ne something special about this storm or I wouldn't be writing about it. This is not the first time something like this had happened to me neither. Almost like a sign from God or some sort of alchemy is the only way I can describe such a moment. Like a perfect moment... It's funny because just this morning I was listening to the radio and people were talking about perfect moments in time. It's quite amazing how the universe has a way of lining up for us in moments you wouldn't think necessary or even possible. Like nature or GOD is talking to you trying to tell you something and your just not sure exactly what it is but desperately want to know.

Within minutes the café almost lost all power from the lightning strikes. The lights were flickering on and off and power surges every 20 seconds. At

THE BOOK OF DEVASTATION

last the back-up generators came on and the power went back to normal. Everyone in the café seemed to be un-disturbed by this coincidence. Start of summer in Florida is all. I have lived in Florida my whole life and storms like this usually aren't so random. Soon after the rain died down and all we were left with was a slight flood and drizzling rain... Yet if you looked in the sky amidst the dark clouds you could see a beautiful magnificent double rainbow. Behind the dark clouds the sunlight was still shining perfectly through to create this perfect moment in time. I had to take a picture and wonder to myself was that storm like some sort of alchemy, a sign from GOD himself for some reason I'm unaware of in the moment. Is there something I'm not seeing that God wants me to see. Was the story I was writing greater than I had once expected? I couldn't but help to think the storm hit the café that day for a good reason. I had no idea at the time the things about myself, that God was anticipating on revealing to me in the up-coming months. I was only as ready as I could have been and had worked so hard to get there.

It was a good story created from a dream I had years ago. Like another creepy pasta story for my great friend Lili. I love listening to her read my stories. I had been clean over a year now so maybe that could have had something to do with all the irony. I Had been feeling very graceful and at peace with myself and God. I felt as if my life was perfectly in lined with God's will, in tuned with the atmosphere and reaching out to the universe for an answer to the chaos that had been swarming around my life for so long now. I had received the gift of the holy spirit and couldn't help but notice the positive energy and spirituality that existed in my everyday life seemed very unreal. Seen and unseen... I can even hear the spirits speaking to me sometimes to. Like the wind is whispering his or her lips for me to hear and believe. I have a brotherly love type bond with my spirit and guardian angel whom all is one I believe. His name is Nelchael. He is most beautiful angel you could imagine and very strong and powerful to a degree um-imaginable. He is the storm...

I believe he's a hybrid angel from heaven who knows both heaven and hell, life and death and because of his hardship in surviving hell has made him most omni-potent! I cry out to him because I know we love each other very much and had hoped it didn't have to be like this. But it's okay. We will always have each other no matter what. My protector... I want to be just like him. Loving and Compassionate to a degree other's cannot comprehend.

It's not always easy seeking, finding, and getting to know your own guardian angel. I had to weed through a lot of crap to find him. I pray God will bless my spiritual life now until forever. I love it and I am super grateful for the life God has provided me with. It said God gives his hardest battles to his strongest warriors. Today I think I'm close to an end or a breakthrough and that's what all these amazing signs in my life are shining towards. I have this one thing trying to hold me back but my spirit will just not allow it. I can see reiki waves channeling negative energy out right from inside and around me. The universe has a higher purpose for my life and is calling out to me to come forth. I see it, and one day at a time, slowly but surely, I will grow towards it until I reach it. I'm not exactly sure what it is I's supposed to do except be patient until I know for sure. Not to mention the Tallis-man spiders that have been cropping up. I took care of those with the fire from God. Times are hard and I want to be financially free like everyone else. Do all the things I always wanted to with this life and live it to the fullest. My childhood was a dream come true but my adulthood has not been so easy making my dream come true for my kids. I'm still young.

Today is Independence-day. My birthday was two days ago. The kids are outside playing with their fireworks while I write. My divine communication. I hope I make it back to heaven one day. I wonder what it would be like now. I have an idea. I read about it in the bible and its sounds magnificent. T'was just a small village from what I remember. I heard somewhere that nothing pays nobody but itself around here. I'm no longer concerned about if I get what I deserve anymore. I'm worth more than what this poor world can offer me all I can do is wish to continue to help in the best way I can. I have already don't so much with so little recognition that I'm used to it. Almost like a slave who has accepted his reality.

No worries I'm completely capable of handling the next step, hurdle, obstacle that may come my way... Life's a beautiful journey even in my dark days. I grow in strength only to have better good days. All sinners are saints who don't give up... I accept myself always in the rest of all my days hopefully forever or until I'm done. Instead of asking ourselves what love is why don't we ask ourselves what this so-called lust is... I have always considered myself to love all of life. Everything is life is worth loving. Life is good because my GOD is so great. Greater than the storm that cross corded my writing that day.

EMPOWERING THE MARINES

Well it was right around the end of the presidential election when I had this unusual dream so I decided to right about it. I was in the process of remembering who I am through recovery and the 12 step basis. I'm a Republican/Democrat who was planning on voting for Donald Trump at the time. Times were quite crucial and it seemed our government elite were in ka-hoots and peace looked grim. I was just getting sober and going through a type of spiritual awakening I had never experienced before. I voted for Trump and a big supporter of constitutional rights.

One night after a long day of recovery I had a dream I was at a strip club waiting to get a lap dance or even laid if I was that lucky, in which case I never really was. She led me back into the V.I.P. room where we both saw another couple having their way with each other and I thought "Whoa," that's like wide open for real! The girl stopped and asked for my money so I gave it to her and she said she would be right back and walked away. I waited awhile uncomfortably and when she didn't come back I thought to myself "some nerve." I came back in front scanning the room looking for her but she was nowhere to be found.

I was then approached by a man wearing a motorcycle jacket and a helmet by his side who said loudly over the music "empower the marines!!" He was obviously an off-duty officer fighting during the crucial times we were living in. Not to mention I had spiritually helped out in the military on some basis, but that's another dream and another story, but maybe these dreams were in some way connected because they did come true. Other than that I'm not sure why he asked me. Maybe because of the song I wrote in dedication to the military some years back. My grandfather was a marine and had just passed on that same week. A lot of irony for me to understand. Was it my spirituality or just a dream?

At first I was naturally upset because he walked away before I could say anything and he seemed a little upset himself. I did what I always seemed to do under pressure, I ran. I went out back to smoke some weed in the woods to try and make sense of everything that had just happened. I was about to cross the stream when I realized something. Our dreams can sometimes have very deep meanings that sometimes should not be taken so lightly like maybe it's more than just a dream and possibly something I should be doing to help or share. Your spirit wants to travel and get out and see and experience new things and while your sleeping is the best time for him to do so. "Namaste," meaning were all connected as one. My spirit or guardian angels' name is Nelchael. We have a great bond and a pure love for one another. I couldn't ask for a better more understanding guardian or keeper. His lightning strike is like none other. Loud, long and deeper than the deepest bass drum. Made up of pure light love and energy. He is a beautiful thing to see. I have only seen him myself a few times in my life but I am one lucky enough to have experienced his true being in reality.

So as I'm hopping over the stream to go have my smoke all of these things are running through my mind and I think "wait, maybe I can help or maybe there's something I can do to help this man." I did a 180 and I ran around the side of the building out front to the parking lot and saw him on his motorcycle almost to the exit about to leave. I was able to flag him down as he saw me at the last second before he left. We were looking for each other in ourselves. He immediately turned around and came racing through the parking lot over to me. Right as he re-approached me we looked each other in the eyes in awe and I woke up. I thought of my grandpa and a tear rolled down my face. Needless to say God was good to America that year. "Don't tread on me," and thou had empowered the marines and a lot of the people with one great song and a dream. Trump won that year although it wasn't easy the military kicked some ass to. In a motion to turn the tables and set everything straight again and stop the madness that had been going on within our own borders. The wool was no longer pulled over the sheep's eyes and the truth began to reveal itself.

MY GUARDIAN ANGEL NELCHAEL'S LETTER ON HOW TO TALK TO GIRLS

tay in the moment. Approach a girl that your attracted to just to see where it goes, I might be pleasantly surprised. Don't read to much into it and don't worry about the coincidence or Déjà vu just talk to her like you normally would. If you want to compliment her than do so and keep it brief. Don't think of others advice is, and go from your own heart and intuition and have fun with it. Either way you will be satisfied in thinking at least you tried. Your single so don't think like its cheating you are free to talk to whatever pretty girl you prefer to talk to, ask for her number or if she would like to come over for dinner. Pray for strength, courage, and guidance. Read upon awakening in the morning you will be a little bit better if you do or even allot better.

ONE MAGICAL MUSHROOM TRIP

So one Spring break weekend, the guys and I planned a Bar-B-Q out at Fort De Soto beach. One of the most grandiose beaches in all of Florida. It is known for its many hidden bunkers, trails, and camp sites, and hidden beaches. A very cool and beautiful place where many tourists do come to visit and then tend to stay. To the guys and I we call this place home. We all grew up here where the Spaniards fought to defend their beach. The old prison bunkers are still there today where the Spaniards would hold and keep their captives. A very historical landmark. You can still find bullet holes inside holding cells in the concrete walls where people used to be executed. Going even further back in history, a destination of the Calhua tribe, there are many old arrowheads to be found at this beach fort as well. A beach with a very long tale of history I might add.

Matt, Rob, Justin, and I went fully prepared and geared for a great time. Plenty of alcohol, weed, and food, plus I had brought a huge bag of mushrooms for a once and a life time trip. The girls out there are always plentiful so we all grilled out at the beach eating and drinking until half the day was up. Around 2 o'clock Justin reminded us how well he knew the old hiking trails at Fort DeSoto beach. We all grasped it to be the perfect adventure for our mushroom trip. When the food and drinks were all gone the guys and I loaded up the trucks and headed out towards the very end of the beach grubbing down our bag of mushrooms on the way.

We arrived half slurred and a bit dizzy, the each of us were. We hung out in the parking lot waiting for the shrooms to kick in and when they did, the psyillosybians hit me like a ton of bricks. Wave after wave like being caught in a hurricane on a boat during a bright and sunny day. I became so naucious I threw up all the mushrooms but it was already set in because now we were all tripping daisies and it was time to get our roll on. We each drank a ton of water at the fountain before making our way through the forest to the most beautiful beach oasis either one of us had ever seen. We were all feeling about as grandiose as the beauty of the beach now, so Matt tied a shirt to the truck antenna just in case we couldn't identify the truck on the way back. Marking our territory like the crew of dogs we are. The hike was now on.

Justin was our crew leader since he was the only crazy son of a bitch who had ever been back there before. Following him through thick and thin and every twist and turn, even when he got lost we trusted he would find his way. And so he did. Hikers passed by gazing upon us a bit awkwardly wondering what was so funny. Maybe it was because there was nothing funny at all that was so funny, and why we were laughing again and again, who knows. The magical mushroom is funny like that. I got stuck looking at a disturbed ant pile that I stepped in for about thirty minutes or so, or at least I thought. I really don't know how long I was looking at that ant pile for but being a bug man on mushrooms, looking at an ant pile I just stepped in while tripping billies and daisies at the same time was about the coolest thing I had ever seen in my life up until then. I can't even begin to explain how cool the trees looked and the angelic feeling we had that day was very nostalgic. Like we too were natives of the origins of this beach in one way or another. Like looking at a trees branches knowing that the roots underneath the ground are mapped just the same as the branches that we see up above the ground. Like looking in a mirror or a glassy lake without the mirror nor lake being there. You can just see it, almost like everything is upside down but right side up... laugh out loud! We were now traveling through our own little world of happiness and beauty.

Out of nowhere just when we thought Justin was lost forever and we would not find our way the end of the trail opening up into a huge Oasis near the beach welcoming us to come and stay. I do believe God granted us a few extra added hours of sunlight this day. This has been by far the most beautiful Oasis I have ever seen in my entire life even to this day. Beautiful perfectly grown rye grass, old ancient yet exotic oak trees so big, providing shade for other wild flowers to grow, and animals to boot, like squirrels, birds, ducks and not to mention the snake were all scared of on the hike in. It was a beautiful sunny day, and we men had just found our own little slice of heaven that day. If I could stay lost in this moment right here forever I would. The kind of Florida summer day a native never forgets. My favorite birds everywhere like bald eagles, sea gulls, egrets, cranes and so on. We walked through this field of grass out onto the edge of the beach where the oak trees grow right up to the beach. Looking now from the edge of the trees on the beach I see a picnic table in the water close enough to swim to and sit on. The waves brushed back and forth over the tables seats and it seemed the tide along with everything else was perfectly adding up that day.

The table had people's names, dates, and nicknames along with love letters carved all over it, and in the near distance out in the channel was a yacht. The yacht looked like it was one of my dreams waiting to come true with about five or six half naked women dancing and listening to music on the front end of it. The guys and I were all in awe. At the moment I didn't know it exactly, and I am just now realizing it as I sit and write this story for the next generation of air-heads. I was already a successful human being the world just didn't know it and either did I. Everyone wants what I have, but everything I have comes from within. The struggle is real but as long as you believe in self and higher self the sky is the limit. And nobody knows where it's going, it just is. Thanks be to God for allowing such wonder and magnanimous proportions of life and blessings all around. We each carved our names in the bench with a knife so that bench would remember us to. Sometimes we just need to open our eyes and our minds a little more to see. I too need help, sometimes every-day, and sometimes I don't get the help I need but I keep on keeping on.

By this next wave I had noticed we were somewhere on Egg-Mont key a well-known fishing spot for many fisher-men like myself. I have passed by this little oasis many times by boat on the way out to go King fishing in the month of August. The mouth of this key empty's out into the deep waters of the Gulf of Mexico. But nothing compares to hiking by foot and seeing the key from within. The guys and I sat there on the bench in the water for some time pondering life and so forth just enjoying each other. Encouraging one another and reminding each other what true friendship is all about. I love my friends very much because of moments shared like this. Its wild to see how past lives can bring great friendships in the present and evermore hopeful ones in the future. That is if you believe in life eternal I suppose. The third eye is like the eye of the universe and those who know how to use or harness it, can bring forth the knowing within.

The time had come to walk back to the truck before sundown. Life was good because it seemed God was really great to us that day. I found what true brotherly love is all about on this adventure. We walked contently back to the truck talking about the ants, the snakes, the trees, birds, women and yachts. We couldn't stop our laughing. The whole trip seemed to be a daisy. Nothing bad about this trip what so ever, except for when Justin lost his way for about a little while. Laugh out loud. Paradise, that only our good friend Justin could find for us. Justin passed away and would be so happy to know I wrote this story for him. He led us through the dark on a bright and sunny day. By far one of the greatest days of my life. I am often asked if I knew when I was going to die what would my last day look like. Well it would look like this only thing I would add would be coming home to my better half. If I had the confidence and knowing I share today I would have swam out to that yacht and claimed it! Still-water a summer day my friends and I will never forget. Sharing spirituality, life, love, and friendship, reminiscing of times like these that we would never forget.

On the drive home we watched the sun go down and realized we possibly had the most tranquil mushroom trip of all time. Moral of the story enjoy every great moment with your friends while growing up because we never get to have as many of these kind of experiences as we would like to. Plus you just never know when you might just lose a great friend so build and create unforgettable memories so you can write about the beautiful times of our lives. The experiences themselves can be worth more than gold or the yacht settled on-top of the water ever so perfectly and anchored out. Amidst everything find your humility. Love doesn't cost a dime when swimming in an oasis with your best friends and a yacht full of half-naked women nearby. Must have been Master P's boat or something. Just a lil insider joke on my part because Only God knows why and today I don't have to ask why. Just keeping it real and the dream boat alive. One day!

LOLA

ike most Friday nights out on the town this one was far from ordinary. It was a first Friday of the month weekend and I had just bought a brand spanking new Hummer H3. Going out on the weekends in the new SUV was a must. First Friday was always a popular party night in my hometown of St. Petersburg FL. Naturally that weekend we all wound up at the bar drinking like it was going out of style.

I got wasted as **** and struck out at the bar. Maybe it was the cocaine and weed on top of all the alcohol that didn't mix well because I was very haggard as my friend Colin would say. I left the bar alone that night but wasn't quite ready to go home so of course I took the new H3 for a ride through the town around 2:30 AM.

I drove down 34th St. also known as US 19 looking for a ****** one that looks good enough for me because I had such a high level of confidence at the time not. Lo and behold it was my lucky night since while I was driving by I saw a good looking figure wearing a short miniskirt nice black skin long hair and a decent sized rack on her. She was walking along the sidewalk. Immediately without hesitation I pulled a U-turn and picked her up. She got right into my new Hummer and before I could speak she said she had a motel room right down the street so off we went to the motel.

We arrived at the cheap motel and without wasting anytime I gave her 20 and she got right down to business sucking me off. I felt a bit awkward but thought it was just the whole night and all that was weird. She began to fully undress for me on the bed and got down on all fours and doggy position. Wearing a condom I proceeded to stick it in from behind and without any lubrication there was some friction there that didn't feel normal to me. I started to catch on and so I did the look around when I did I saw a **** about the same size as my own I wanted to knock him out.

I jumped off her quickly or him and with my pants down around my ankles I fell back into the chair sitting behind me. I commands the bus up in my sack of weed and hopes to smoking some sense into myself. I packed a fat bowl and smoked it with the guy I thought it was a girl. I had some questions so I asked how do you have *****? She I mean he said in a very feminine voice I take estrogen pills I shave everything and wear makeup and a wig on it or extensions etc. Thankfully to say he goes through a lot of trouble to be a girl for people.

Instead of the weed bringing me to my senses I thought well nobody will ever know plus I already paid him I'm wasted and don't feel like jerking off in my own tears when I get home. So **** it hurry up let's finish this up so I can go! I ****** as quickly as possible and got my white *** the hell out of there as quickly as possible without anyone knowing or seeing. Supposedly ** *** was going to Miami in the morning and I was just happy to know ** *** was leaving my town the little trick that he was. I drove home as quickly and safely as possible and passed out with the idea in my head that I would keep it a secret forever. This memory haunted me and my sexuality for years before I realized I'm not gay it had me questioning myself I was afraid of what people would think or say if they found out and I didn't want to keep living with the secret. So I told my cousin Donnie this story at work one day and he about died laughing.

My cousin still makes fun of me today for it all these years later. I laugh with him for the **** **** I used to do when I was young and still hope that one day he may just forget about it but he doesn't. Now every time I hear the song Lola I think of myself as a new man with more experience! I managed to keep it a secret for years and man what a relief it was for me to finally get it out in the open. They say we're only as sick as our secrets. I don't like living with secrets that aren't healthy for me. And trust I do have plenty. And those years I kept it a secret I just could not forget and the struggle was for sure a real one. Life was not easy living with that in the back of your mind all the time. The secret made everything about my life more difficult thinking about it all the time around people wanting to say something about it and not. It's a good locker room story and all my friends always laugh every time they hear it or when someone new hears the story. Since I came clean there has been no shame in my game period in the end it made for a hell of a good laugh and some self introspection. Just for the record I'm not gay! Just sabotaged! Come on go you!

CROSSING PATHS WITH MY FAIRY GOD MOTHER

here to begin as some of you may already know I'm an addict and alcoholic and have been battling this disease since I was about 17 years old. It is said God gives his toughest battles to his strongest warriors. I stay strong through my struggles. No cakewalk overcoming addiction. Where some can take it or leave it addicts have a more difficult time moderating. Praying about it works for me and it does help tremendously I am precise when I pray be open minded and then wait on God's good graces.

By the time I was 31 years old I was almost two years sober I had weathered through much hardship to get to where I was going when I got there and unexpectedly went through a lot of anger pain grief and jealousy It was like a period of mourning where I was very emotional I thought I had lost my girlfriend forever but she is still in the picture which has helped my heart tremendously knowing that she is still around.

I relapsed on my drug of choice methamphetamines the same day I got paid. Complacent and plugged back in from an X problem junkie.

The plan was to use just one more time but it snowballed into more and more like it always does. I broke my hand in a fight defending myself from my so-called friend who couldn't take no for an answer. I got away and went back home with my drugs I got high as soon as I got home which quite possibly could have been my last fix. I was lying in my bed completely shell shocked at once I saw my whole spirit leave my body and hover toward the ceiling looking down on me. my light and love from within. the source of energy that keeps me Alive. The gift of the Holy Spirit.

At this very instant I begin to see this beautiful pink eye gazing at me from the middle of the room moving around scarcely and keeping a close watch on me. It was the most beautiful thing my two eyes had ever seen in my entire existence. It was my third eye from what I understand and very scary to see. Next as I feel someone standing over me pouring out a bag of invisible snakes over top of me lying in bed. I could feel them yet I could not see the. right when I thought I couldn't take it anymore and I was going to give up on hope she showed up. My fairy godmother appeared before I even knew it she was there. I look up to my ceiling and up to my surprise in the corner of my bedroom closest to my bed right above me to the right she was there fluttering gracefully. She was wearing a pink dress and her bright pink aura shined all around her and I. She had Hummingbird like wings on her back and at about this time I wish I had a witness and thought why do these things always happen to me when I'm alone. She was about 6 inches by 6 inches and hovered there fluttering back and forth shining this most beautiful pink aura I've never seen anything like it before in my entire life I thought maybe I was delusional because of the drugs but the experience was way too real to think it was fake I was undergoing some sort of transformation I don't expect anyone to believe it to be a true story but I will leave it open to interpretation. She was beautiful and tiny she gave me comfort and peace whispering to me and letting me know it will be OK. God bless our hearts because she was my hope my light and my love at that night. Saving my life she was. My peace and my strength, I knew it was going to be OK.

As I felt the bag of invisible snakes being poured over my head and slithering all around me and through my bed I was still alive and awakened and jumped up quickly to find nothing in my bed but me. She was still there hovering above me in the corner of my room floating back and forth and forth and back. She looked a lot like the pink fairy godmother in the TV series "Once Upon a time" but in real life. The snakes were still there slithering around my comforter yet I could not see them and they soon went away. With her wand waving and voice whispering she gave me an overwhelming sense of peace and comfort and a scared moment that only she had the power to provide such a transformation for me. I can't remember exactly how she left but after some time and peace and quiet once I was settled she flew away and disappeared. It was like she filled me back up with light and love and returned it to my body. A new spirit perhaps. She healed me and blessed me with an omnipotent source of light and love.

The next day I got an e-mail from this beautiful lady dressed in pink, offering me a free tarot card reading. I accepted and we both knew that we had not crossed paths like this for no reason. I eagerly accepted the reading and she reassured me of who I was most importantly my love and success. She has been my medium ever since. She was spot on with all of her drawings readings and predictions. Being in a rough spot in my journey I did my best to follow her suggestions. A day later my girlfriend Patricia and I found out she is getting her father's inheritance and that we were going to be able to live better more abundant lives together.

Life can really surprise you sometimes after all my struggles and hardships it seemed the hard work and all my creativity was finally starting to pay off in more than one way. My gifts from God allowed me to be a blessing to our world and to tell my story. I aided in finding a solution to my alcoholism through working with God and friends and brought some truth to the world. I believe God has greater plans for my life has filled me with his Holy Spirit and will not leave me alone. God has always been there for me and when others weren't. A great thing to rely on or fall back on all you need is a little bit of faith and anything is possible. The sky really is the limit. I've so always kept God close to my heart.

Houdini lived his whole life hoping and searching to witness such miracles and have such a experience and did not.It's a reminder of how important I am to the universe even when I may not think that I am. I too have suffered from a low self esteem something that for the most part I have overcome through walking in grace humility and acceptance. I have had many spiritual experiences that I can remember. I have had out of body experiences and performances and have shared in spirit.

One time I brought home with me a set of wind chimes as a souvenir and a reminder that it really happened from one such event, miraculous is the only way I could explain it. I stored them in my hockey bag when I got home where I knew I would find them later down the road as a token of good cheer. When I found the wind chimes I was like yes right where I left them. It was evidence to myself that the flight actually took place. Miraculous.

I wound up in a house I designed in high school and even helped paint it and some exterior yard work before I moved in. It's just wonderful how the universe works in my life. More approved the universe lines up things precariously for a reason. I could go on and on about different experiences but this one was by far the most compelling. The spirit likes to play with me from time to time like pulling my hose outside when nobody is around late at night. One night the spirit tapped my wind chimes at night and even feet sweeps me on my ass when I'm not paying much attention. I have also seen the spirit put a 25% discount tag on a pair of board shorts

I wanted while standing in line at the store. Needless to say that sign wasn't there before I saw him put it there for me so I might as well buy them too. It's a good deal what the heck right. That's what I said to myself.

Yes the spirit has been good to me. Good karma for being a great person and giving much of myself to the world around me. My friend and our love. Life is good and I have grown. The story reminds me of the song tiny dancer.